EcstAgony

A Homosexual, Sadomasochistic, Transitional Journey

A Novel
by
Sphen Kari

"For there are some eunuchs, which were so born from *their* mother's womb; and there are some eunuchs, which were made eunuchs of men: and there be eunuchs, which have made themselves eunuchs for the kingdom of heaven's sake. He that is able to receive *it*, let him receive *it*." – Jesus The Christ KJV of the *Holy Bible*, Matthew 19:12

(An explicit sexual novel – Definitely not for anyone who has not reached the age of maturity).

Published by:
Alexis Publications
Stone Mountain, Georgia
www.alexispublications.com

Library of Congress Catalog Card Number: TXu 1-571-679
ISBN 13: 978-0-9800667-0-8
ISBN 10: 0-9800667-0-0

First Printing: June 2008

Printed in the U.S.A.

Chapter I

Max could hardly wait for Kimberly and Brian to be off, as he hurriedly placed their luggage in the trunk of the sedan.

"Don't give your mama no crap," he said to his son, teasingly, trying to contain his anxiety. "You may be a natural born ball player, joker, but you're no driver, yet!" His hand on top of his son's head, he was mauling it, playfully.

Then, he went to the driver's side.

"I wish you would come with us," Kimberly pled.

"She don't want to see me," Max said, talking about Kimberly's mother. "You and Brian will be just fine. I'll figure out something to do around here to keep me busy. I'm thinking about shaving," he said, fingering his mustache.

"Would that be too much to ask for?" Kimberly smiled as they kissed goodbye. He watched as she backed out of the garage.

Then, they were gone.

No sooner was the car out of sight did Max take out his phone. He dialed *her* number before he got back into the house he shared with Kimberly and their son.

Breathing a sigh of relief when she answered, he said, "I'll be there in 45 minutes.... I'm shaving my mustache!"

* * * *

The first time, Max had gotten totally wiped out before he could let her do what she had been urging him to let her do since they first met—use a strap-on on him. The first time he submitted to her urging was a month ago. He had both drank and smoked, something he had long given up, until then. Then, he let her do it to him. And when she did, to his amazement, he experienced an excitement and pleasure like none he had ever experienced before! Afterwards, he had taken her the same way she had taken him while she still wore the strap-on. Both times he had exploded with such force he feared he wouldn't stop cumming!

And then there was the time after that, and the time after that, like now, he found himself anxiously wanting her to take him that way. Though, he couldn't admit to her that was what he wanted—nor could he admit it to himself.

"Mmmmm, nice!" Sharon said, caressing his cheek as he came through the door. "You really did shave it off."

She closed and locked the door behind him.

"Uh-huh," he said.

They kissed.

"Probably for the best," she murmured, as she hung-up his jacket.

"Huh?" Max asked.

"Oh… nothing…. Want to make us a drink?"

He always drank Bloody Marys, and he made this one extra strong. So, at first when he got blindingly drunk, he thought it was the gin. He didn't notice it when Sharon made the third round, and dissolved the powder in his.

Soon, he lay stretched out on Sharon's big, king-size bed, naked, face down.

"I'm going to make it oooh soooo good for you tonight, baby!" she purred. "I've got something real special for you," Sharon whispered in his ear while she bound his wrists with the scarf, softly, lightly, the way he had done to her—and she had done to him—a few times before. Then, he let her tie his bound wrists to the headboard, so that his arms and hands were over his head.

She loved the mellow, close-eyed smile of surrender she saw on his face whenever she was about to take him this way. She had seen that type of smile on a man's face before. And she felt she knew what it meant. His contented mien afterwards had been all she needed to arrange tonight's event.

Soon, Max's head was not only spinning from that last drink, but even more so from his growing anticipation. She was massaging his neck, shoulders and back, and now she was naked too, and straddling him.

"Baby, I'm going to give you what you *really* want, tonight," she whispered. Moving down his body with her lips, she was kissing his lower back and his buns.

2

And, without his noticing, she was motioning for the three shirtless and shoeless men in the doorway to come in. She had kept them hidden downstairs, so Max hadn't seen them.

"This is going to be soooo good, baby... just what I know you've been wanting!" she murmured.

Quietly, removing their pants, momentarily all three men were naked.

The smaller one was first to mount Max. Sharon, who was still massaging and kissing him, lifted herself up now, and the smaller man took her place. Only, he was turned facing Max's butt, and instantly he was massaging and licking his buns. Pulling them apart, he sent his tongue down to his anus, making Max's body shudder, and a loud sigh escape his throat.

Still naked and silently directing them, Sharon picked up a camcorder and began taping the show.

The other two guys had Max's legs, holding them apart. One had his other hand underneath Max, gripping his cock, while the other guy was massaging his balls.

"Oohhhh! God! What's happening?! Wha . . .?" Max asked, loudly moaning his awe and erotically delirious excitement. He sighed, loudly, when the smaller one licked and sucked hard and long on his anus with loud, smacking sounds!

"You like that, don't you, baby?" Sharon whispered. She too was excited by Max's cries and moans, and by watching his body squirm and pulsate in erotic submission. "You like having your ass licked and sucked like that, don't you?!"

"Yeessss," Max moaned in his ecstasy.

He was somewhat bewildered at hearing her so close to his ear. He knew something was different, but under the affect of the drinks, in the darkened room with his eyes closed, he couldn't allow himself to comprehend what was happening to him.

Is...? Is this real...? Am I dreaming?! The questions danced in his mind. Then, he heard her, again.

"Yeesss baby, and tonight your ass's gonna get exactly what you really want, baby! You're gonna get some real hard fucking dicks fucking your ass, tonight!"

She passed a plastic, baby oil-filled syringe to the smaller one, who moved himself around between Max's thighs. Parting his hard, tight, quivering buns, he inserted it, as Sharon focused in on Max's anus filming up close as the syringe entered it. The shot was crystal clear when the smaller one pumped the oil into

3

him. Then, he rolled the condom onto his own hard, cock, and immediately sent it into Max's waiting, lube-seething anus.

"Oohhhh...aaahhhhhh!" Max threw his head back and cried out as he felt the hard cock enter.

"You like that, baby?!" Sharon asked, coaxingly.

"Aahhhhh...mmmm...yesss," Max sighed.

"I know what you want, baby. I knew you'd like it! You been wanting a real, hard dick in that tight-ass pussy of yours for a long time, haven't you?!" Sharon insisted.

"Mmmmm.... Aaahhhhhh! Yeesss!" he sighed, in response to his own pleasure, as much as in answer to Sharon's question.

Is it?!.... Is it... r-e-a-l?! He wondered.

Still, he couldn't allow himself to believe he was actually being taken by a man.

"Well...that's what you've got, baby...that's what I've got for you tonight! All night long, baby. I've got two more waiting for your tight ass!"

And even as she said it, his mind still couldn't grasp what she meant.

"Don't let him cum! Don't let him cum!" Sharon urged, not wanting Max to cum with the smaller one. "Get the ring on his cock, dam-mit!" she ordered, in a domineering voice Max had never heard before.

One of them slid his hand underneath pulling Max's meaty, hard cock down between his legs, and snapped a plastic ring around it and his balls. He squeezed the ring, making it tight enough to cut off every drop of the clear liquid that had been streaming from the bulging head of Max's hard cock.

Max found he couldn't stop moaning not only from the pounding he was receiving, but now from the pain the ring was causing as well.

Soon, the smaller one was sighing and moaning, too, wildly thrusting himself in and out of Max.

Moaning loudly, he came, in the condom, deep in Max's anus.

In an erotically-ecstatic state like none he had ever known—suddenly, Max knew!

4

He didn't want to believe it! He wanted to hate the helplessly erotic way he was feeling. But, he couldn't. Because, he could clearly hear a man say:

"Let me have some of that, man! It looks so mutha-fuckin' hot… and tight! I want to get me some of this!"

It was the one who had put the cock-ring on him. He was pushing the smaller one aside and mounting Max with his hard, condom-clad cock. His was not only longer than the one before, but it was as meaty as Max's.

"Shit! Get'em up on his knees!" he ordered. The other two managed to wedge a couple of pillows underneath Max. And, in one fail swoop, the second one penetrated Max's anus as far as he could go.

"Oohhhhhhh!" Max cried out not from the intense arousal he was experiencing, but also from the instant, nauseating pain he felt from knowing he was being taken by a man—and he liked it!

"They're gonna break your tight ass in, tonight, baby!" Sharon promised.

"Oohhhhh, it's too big!" he cried in protest. "Uuhhhh… It hurts!"

"Yeah, but you can take it! You can take it, baby; it's the same size I've been using on you!" she said to him. Then, to the others, "Get him on his side and suck his dick!"

Max had 6 inches of an 8 inch cock in him and his cock had a ring on it while it was being sucked; he wanted to believe he was dreaming. He had never told a soul, that when he was younger he had often wondered what it would feel like to be fucked by a guy with a big cock and sucked at the same time. Now, somewhere in the back of his mind, he knew he was experiencing it. He knew he was enjoying it. He knew this was real. And, being bound, drunk and drugged, he knew he could do nothing to stop it—even if he wanted to.

"This ass's sooo fuckin' tight, baby!" the one taking him now was murmuring, while holding his buns apart and rhythmically ramming his cock in and out of him. "Mmmm …mmmm… mmmm!" he moaned each time he rammed himself into Max. "This some good… mmmm... tight-ass… mmmm... pussy, baby! Good … tight ass-pussy!"

Both he and Max were moaning when the third one, whose hard, 10-inch cock was evidence of his growing excitement, decided it was his turn!

"Oohhhhh! Oohhh-aahhh … aahhhhh!" Max moaned, "I want to cum! Let me cum... Pleas…."

"Not yet, baby!" Sharon said, still videotaping the action. "Not yet!"

"Wha...?! What're you doin' to me?!" he asked, panting breathlessly.

"I'm giving you what you want! You know you want it! It's good ... isn't it?! Isn't this what you want?!"

"Mmmm... aahhhh . . . ! You fuckin' me?!" he managed to ask.

"Oh, I'm fucking your ass, all right, baby!" Sharon said. "Ain't it good?!"

"Yessss!" he sighed, delirious. "Mmmmm!"

"And I'm gonna fuck it all night, baby! I'm gonna fuck your ass all night long!"

Now the 10-incher was ready. He slipped the condom onto his big, rock-hard cock, and slapped the 8-incher's ass who was still taking Max as he said: "Come on, nigga, it's time for me to get some of this!"

"Ooooh! Oohhhhh! Aaahhhhh!" Max's 8-incher cried out from the slap. "Do it again! Slap my ass again, baby ... make me cum!" he cried, as he egged the 10-incher on. The 10-incher obliged him, slapping his buns over and over again—until he came in the condom like the first one, deep in Max's lube-oozing anus.

Among these three, it was obvious that the 10-incher was the leader by virtue of the size of his manhood, alone. Now, he positioned himself to take his part in the train on Max. Working with his thumbs, he massaged the small, oozing opening, working his thumbs in deeper. Using his thumbs he held Max's anus open, and in an instant, buried the large head of his cock inside it!

"Mmmm! Oohhhh...." Max grunted and cried out.

"This is 10 inches, baby!" Sharon whispered excitedly into his ear. "Ten inches! And, he's gonna fuck your ass all night ... and you're gonna take every inch of it, tonight!"

Max heard that dominatrix voice, again. He felt his head spinning. Every nerve in him was firing! He felt like he would explode from the pressure of the hard rod stuffing him. And, slipping slowly in and out of consciousness, Max wouldn't remember much after that point.

But Sharon was true to her words. She videotaped it all while he was rubbed, licked, sucked, beaten and fucked for the rest of the night.

When they finished and it was over, they dressed him and drove him home. It was before daybreak, the next morning.

6

* * * *

Max was awakened by bright sunlight shining on his handsome, dark face. He was in his driveway behind the steering wheel of his car. He knew where he was—and he knew where he had been. Now he was feeling light-headed and seeing double. He was glad Brian and Kimberly were not at home; he wouldn't have to explain anything. He knew he had a day to recuperate.

He drove the car on into the garage. Then he went inside. Though the telephone message light was blinking, he knew he didn't want to talk to anyone. He didn't want to think about anything. So, fully-clothed, he fell across the bed, and slept.

Max was 36 years old. He was the type of man who never had trouble attracting women. Good-looking, intelligent, educated and a bit refined, his bearing and his clothes made his conservative up-bringing evident. He and Kimberly had been together for over 11 years, now. He knew she loved him and he had grown comfortable and secure in her love. He knew that all she wanted from him was for him to be there. And he knew that she knew he would never marry her.

Five hours later, he awoke to the buzzing of the mobile phone in his pocket. Fumbling around, he found the phone and saw the name and number. Sharon had left a message. He pushed the message button.

"Hello, darling. I thought you would have called by now! I know you've looked at your DVD... star! I hope you aren't too upset with me. But you got to experience that dream you told me about—remember? And you made a little money! Call me!"

His mind was crystal clear now.

Listening to her, he knew exactly what she was talking about. He instinctively rubbed his butt, as the knowledge of the night before made him quiver and sigh. Was he angry? Should he be angry? Had he listened to his body, he would have known the answer to the questions that filled his head. Just then he noticed the blinking telephone message light, again. He hit the button.

"Darling, do look at the DVD alone ... I mean, like, all by yourself. We wouldn't want the wrong people to see it, now, would we? Enjoy the money. You earned it. Let me know what you think!" Sharon's voiced beamed through the machine.

Suddenly, he was confused. What DVD? What money? Then, he spotted the envelope in the pocket of the jacket he had thrown across a chair when he first

7

got home. He took it out. Five, one-hundred dollar bills floated to the floor. He caught the DVD before it fell. Max hesitated before popping the disk into the player. For an instant he knew that this could change everything. He inserted the disk.

Then, he sat on the bed and watched the show from the night before—his show.

On the screen he saw them—all three of them. He watched them suck, beat, rub, squeeze and fuck him, again and again and again. He watched them stick the lube-filled-syringe into him. He watched them sucking his cock and balls, and licking and sucking his ass. He watched them put the ring on his hard, throbbing cock. And, he watched the first one mount and enter him. Then the next. He watched the 10-incher drive his huge, hard cock into him, while beating his right bun so hard he was sure it blistered. Soon, Max was breathing hard. Looking at the video, he had become as hard as a rock, and he was stroking himself. On the screen the 10-incher was slapping his buns and steadily driving his huge cock deeper into him, until his big balls were slapping against his ass. Max came while he watched one of the three take the ring off his cock, and his cum oozed out hot onto his fingers as the man gulped it down on the screen.

An ocean of emotions washed over him as he lay there panting heavily watching the film again. He felt helpless. He felt trapped. He felt forced. He felt guilty. But, the main thing he felt, and the feeling that kept overtaking him was sheer, erotic pleasure. And though he didn't like himself for feeling that way, he couldn't stop watching the video and he couldn't stop the feeling.

He was still watching it when the telephone rang. It startled him. Instinctively he clicked the power button turning the TV off.

"Babbbyyy, why haven't you called me?" Sharon chimed.

"I fell asleep," Max answered, dryly.

"Well, did you get your gift?" she asked. "Or, should I say… the moolah? After all, your ass earned it!"

"Yeah," Max replied. "You let them niggas run a train on me!"

"Yeah, baby! And I could see how much you liked it. Wasn't it good?! In the video, couldn't you see how much you enjoyed it … couldn't you?!" she insisted.

"I was drunk! I didn't…. It was supposed to be me and you, Sharon! I didn't know what was happening!" Max said, a bit too defensively.

"Baby, didn't you tell me all men wonder what it would be like to be fucked by some guy with a big dick? Well, now you know! And, you know it feels good.

That's why I let you fuck me like that, and that's why you let me! Because, it feels so good."

The last thing he had seen on the screen was her taking him with the strap-on.

"Now, didn't you tell me that?" she continued.

"I didn't say I wanted to be *fucked* by a man!" Max exclaimed.

"Men, baby. And, no you didn't. But, you're a man, aren't you?! And besides, didn't you want it… just a little…? I mean … wasn't it gooood?" she purred.

He didn't answer.

"Have you looked at the DVD?" she asked.

"I just finished looking at it."

"Well, you can see that it was all good, baby. You can make some money, now. You made a little last night … but now you can make a lot! And the way they were going at that tight ass of yours... they loved it! I knew they'd be back."

Max gave a cynical chuckle. "Be back? For what?!" he questioned, indignantly, as if he didn't know.

"For some more of your good stuff, baby," Sharon said.

"I don't think so," Max replied, stingingly.

Now, it was Sharon who laughed.

"Oooohhh, come on, baaby. They're discrete," she said. "But they already have you on tape taking it in the ass. And you wouldn't want that disk to end up in the wrong hands, would you? So you may as well make some money with it, baby. Have fun!"

"*Blackmail*?!" Max said, angrily. Resigned.

"I'm trying to help you … in a way … with something I thought you'd like," Sharon protested. "But yes, actually, I don't think they are above that."

Again, he didn't respond.

"Okay, look, how about if I try to get you more money. They want you again tomorrow night. They said, after dark. They said, if you're working with us, it

9

won't take all night. Otherwise…. Anyway, I was told to make you an offer… an offer you can't refuse, as they say," she said, and chuckled, ironically.

"Oh yes, I can refuse that shit!" Max retorted, sarcastically.

"Oh! Come on, Max! Baby, you must have liked it! I mean, you were doing everything except asking for it … and that was because you were too drunk to talk! I'm telling you, these guys know a lot of people. They could take it to one of their parties… or, to somebody else's party and who knows, maybe somebody who knows you could be there, you know? People you wouldn't want to ever see it. "

"That's blackmail!" he exclaimed again, more heatedly.

"Yes. Okay. But darling, I do hope you'll get over it and see the benefit of making the money, and having fun with it!"

Max hung up the phone. His mind was reeling: *I could lose everything—never teach again… Kimberly… Brian! God! What to do?!*

Had he listened to his body, he would have known what he would do.

Still, with sober, somber thoughts filling his head, he didn't know. Rubbing the side of his temple, Max slowly sat down on the side of the bed and, thoughtlessly, his finger hit the button on the TV remote. On the screen, the 10-inch cock was ramming into him, and the camera was close up on the action. He couldn't stop the stirring in his loins, yet again. He felt weak. Lying back on the bed, he couldn't stop looking at it. And, he couldn't stop the feeling consuming his entire being well after the video ended.

* * * *

Sharon was not surprised when she opened the door for Max the next night. They had only spoken that one time since the last time he was there, but she knew he would come.

"Hello, baby! Come on in. I'm really glad you came. We couldn't do this without you," she said in her sing-song voice, opening the door, wide.

"Oh, so we're a comedian all of a sudden," Max said, dryly, removing his jacket.

"Oohhhh… lighten up, Max!" Sharon responded, taking his jacket. "You want a drink or something?"

"Yeah… something. What you got?" he asked, demandingly.

Sharon motioned to the tray on the coffee table. "What do you want?" she asked.

Wanting and not wanting what was about to happen to him—and wanting the money—Max had told himself, *I had to come*. He knew that Sharon was perfectly capable of carrying out the threat about showing the DVD. *Didn't she arrange the train and tape it?*, he said to himself.

It took two Bloody Marys and a row of cocaine in each nostril before he felt ready to give himself to Sharon and her boys. The three men stayed out of sight until Sharon got him naked, bound his wrists with a scarf, and tied him up like before. Then, they made their presence known.

Sharon was kissing and sucking his body, and Max's head was already spinning when the others joined them. Now, he could feel their hands and mouths on him as well. They were lifting him, placing his naked, limp body face down across a wedge something that made his ass easily accessible. Only his head, knees and legs rested on the bed, now.

"You've got 3 mouths on you, baby. You feel that?" he heard Sharon purr up close to his ear, as one sucked Max's cock, one sucked his balls, and a third one rimmed his anus. "How does that feel?" she asked, excitedly.

"Mmmmm!" Max's long, soulful sigh filled the air as he felt himself being consumed by the ecstasy of their mouths. His sighs and moans spoke the words he couldn't say.

After licking and sucking his anus with his agile tongue, the 6-incher was once again allowed to take him first.

"I know it feels good, baby! See..." Max heard Sharon whisper. "... All you've got to do is just let it feel good!"

Though Max couldn't reply, he couldn't contain the sighs and moans that were escaping from his throat. He took the wild, climatic-thrusts of the first one, until again he came just like before.

Again the 8-incher was next. He pushed his hard cock into Max until his balls were slapping against Max's, and while Melvin, the 10-incher, was beating his ass like before.

All the while Sharon was taping the action, constantly moving and positioning herself to get up close and personal.

Max was Melvin's for the rest of the evening. After he had worked his 10-inch cock all the way into Max, on his knees, he made the others remove the wedge and he turned over onto his back, holding Max tightly atop him. Max's back was to Melvin's belly. Holding Max's legs apart with his legs, Melvin still had his cock buried in him. He let the other two take turns sucking his cock and balls for the camera. And when they were done, without dislodging himself, he came to his knees. Lifting Max's ass up off the bed, he put Max's legs over his shoulders and grasping each thigh to his chest, tightly, Melvin took him from the front like he was taking a woman.

With his hands bound over his head, the other two securing his legs over Melvin's shoulders, and Melvin's 10-inch cock pulsating, rhythmically, deep within him, Max could only lay there, stoned, taking it, moaning, wanting it to end, yet not.

At 12:45 a.m., Max found himself pulling into his garage. Stoned, he turned off the engine, and slept in the car.

* * * *

The next morning, Brian and Kimberly found him there when it was time for him to take his son to school.

"I don't know what's wrong with you!" from a sleepy haze, Max heard Kimberly's angry voice. Brian had jumped in the car. "I thought I was going to have to take him to school, because no one knew you were out here sleeping in the car!" she exclaimed. Her anger was evident on her face and in her voice.

"Why are you sleeping in the car, daddy?" Brian asked.

"I ... uh.... I got back so late, I didn't want to wake up the whole house," Max said, straightening himself up in the driver's seat.

"I smell alcohol!" Kimberly continued. "You gonna be able to take him to school?"

"Yes! Yeah," Max said, "I'll take him.... I can drive." He was starting the engine.

"Well... be careful, won't you?" she said, looking at Max suspiciously now. "I've got to get to work. I'll see you guys this evening," she added, and watched as Max backed the car out of the garage, slowly.

12

Driving along Max's mind was filled with thoughts of the night before. His body was tightening as memories flooded his head. And as he was remembering, his body was again experiencing how it had been used only hours before.

He was consciously working at maintaining control of his body, barely hearing his son's childish rambling until he exclaimed,

".... Daddy! Daddy! Is this enough money to send me to baseball camp?"

Max looked to see his son holding up five crisp one hundred dollar bills.

"That's not quite enough, son," he said, calmly taking the money from his boy who looked heart-broken at hearing this. "But I'll get enough. Anything for my boy," he added, and tossed his son's head playfully, making him smile once more.

When his son got out of the car and ran into the school building, Max looked for and found the new DVD. He could hardly wait to get home to look at it. He could no longer control his burgeoning cock.

At home, he came on the bed while viewing the new DVD and beating his meat. Then he showered. Coming out, he tied a towel around his waist and tucked it. While towel drying his hair, he called Sharon.

"Hello darling."

"I need to make $2,000.00 by week after next," he said.

"I think you can do that. I know a place where you can make it in a day."

"And where's that?" he asked, purposefully making himself sound bland, though his interest was piqued.

"I'm told that it's a beautiful place where you can make $2,000.00 a day just laying around and...."

"And being fucked," he said, flatly.

"Of course. That's what it's all about, baby."

"Where is it?"

"We're not allowed to know. Melvin and the others know. Anyway, he's already talking about getting you there. That's how I know you can make a lot of money, if that's what you want. After seeing you on tape, baby, he told me his peeps up there are asking for your ass! You want me to call him?"

"I want two thousand a day!"

"Okay. I'll tell him that. I'll call you back."

He hung up the telephone.

He stood there for a minute thinking about what she said: "… they're asking for your ass… two thousand a day…." He told himself it didn't matter. And now, it was easy for him to convince himself of that because he needed the money for Brian. He told himself he would do this one more time. Then he would leave it—and Sharon. He told himself that as he changed the bed linen, and then he fell across the clean-smelling bed and slept.

Chapter II

"What did you tell her?" Sharon asked.

"That they want to see if I'm fit to do some reserve duty," Max replied, simply, and took a hit of cocaine.

Sharon laughed out loud at that.

"That's about right!" she said. "How long did you say you'll be gone?"

"Five … maybe six days."

"Good, baby. I'll put your car in the back, since they'll bring you back here."

He gave her the keys, and snorted another row. He took several more hits of cocaine while she was gone to move his car. By the time she returned, the drug was taking an affect. He was feeling good.

"You know I'm doing this because I need the money," he said. Taking the drink she was offering him, he sat back and kicked off his shoes.

"Of course, darling," she replied, seeing his condition. She turned on the television.

Max's latest video was playing. On the screen Max was buck-naked lying on his back on top of Melvin, who was using his legs to hold Max's legs apart, and whose cock was just about disappearing into Max. On the television one had his cock and balls in his mouth, while the other was licking and sucking his nipples. Max went silent looking at it, and if he was trying to contain his arousal, he was unsuccessful.

With drink in hand now Sharon came to him and sat on the floor next to his legs. Slowly sending her hand up his leg, she watched him watching the video, and could see from the bulge in his pants that he had an urge he couldn't contain. By the time her hand reached its goal, the tip of his meaty, hard cock was already soaking wet.

She felt she had done the right thing.

She had seen the possibility in Max when she first met him some two months ago in the grocery store. She was drawn to him initially by his looks, looks she found somewhat familiar, and very pleasing. The first time she had let him come to her place, he had made it clear that his initial attraction to her was her big, round, beautiful ass.

"I want to do it to you in your ass," he had said that first time.

She had smiled. "Only if I can do it to you..." she had replied, and smoothly added: "in yours."

His surprise had been evident on his face. His smile had been dreamy—as if trying to imagine what that would truly feel like.

He had said, "Okay."

Now, realizing what she was doing, he lifted himself to let her pull his pants down. He closed his eyes and threw his head back as her mouth engulfed him and he felt the hard, pulling sucks drawing him, making him even harder if that could be. Then, he felt the cock-ring go on at the base of his cock. On the underside, this one had a marble-size steel ball on it that immediately stopped the flow of his juices.

In the video, Melvin had placed Max's legs over his shoulders and was plunging in and out of him. Without knowing how, soon he realized he was naked and Sharon was binding his wrists with a scarf. Naked, with his wrists bound, he didn't stop Sharon when she placed the silk scarf over his eyes, and tied it behind his head. Coming around in front of him, Sharon placed the drink to his mouth and forced him to drink it down. Then, she guided him to the bed where she tied his bound wrists to the headboard.

As soon as he was secure, the three were upon him. But this time only Melvin entered him, while the other two licked and sucked every inch of him all the way to the Lodge.

Max could hear his own sighs, cries and moans as they took him. But, he couldn't tell whether the sounds were coming from him or from his video. Like he wanted, the cocaine and whatever Sharon had put in his drink had sent him into that helpless state where all he could do was feel the hard cock pumping in and out of him, and the hot mouths. All he could hear were his own cries and moans of ecstasy. Slipping in and out of consciousness, he had no knowledge of being taken to the Lodge, even as the cock was planted in him and the mouths continued to consume his every inch.

And, when Melvin finally exploded deep within him, in that spot, he did remember feeling a hot, quivering within like nothing he had ever felt before.

"Aahhhh! Gooddd! Pleaseeee let me cum!" he heard himself crying pleadingly.

He felt the cock-ring being loosened. Instantly, he felt his cum coursing through and out of him with such force, he could hear and feel the one sucking his cock gulping down mouthfuls! Soon, slipping in and out of a sweet nothingness, everything faded to black.

Only to be awaken to the sounds of his own moans and sighs, still!

It took him a minute to realize the sounds were coming from an overhead television playing the video from the night before. He didn't know whether it was morning or still dark. He lay on his back. He realized he was naked, save for the loosen cock-ring, and lying on silk sheets on a bed in a lavishly gaudy, well-lit bedroom. He was no longer bound.

His hands were rubbing the smoothness that he was laying upon, when he noticed Melvin, robed and sitting in a chair underneath the television, staring at him.

"So, you've finally come around," Melvin said, now coming and sitting next to where Max lay on the bed.

It was the first time Max had actually seen him other than in the videos. It was the first time he had ever spoken to him. He was surprised at how normal he looked and sounded when he wasn't fucking him.

He was fairer than Max, well-proportioned, about 6'1", and rather slim. His hair was in corn-rows all gathered in the back in a plait on his neck.

The knock at the door came almost as soon as he sat down.

"I thought I was going to have to have breakfast without you," he said. He let his hand brush Max's thigh as he got up and opened the door.

The waiter who pushed the cart into the room was young. Max thought he had a Hispanic look about him, with straight dark hair and lashes. He wore what looked like a cook's uniform, without the hat. He didn't really look at Max or Melvin the brief while he was in the room.

"Would you like me to serve?" he asked Melvin, his accent confirming Max's thought.

"I'll take it from here. Thanks," Melvin replied, and the waiter backed out of the room.

Melvin lifted a lid and found scrambled eggs. Holding the lid, he looked at Max and said, "Looks good, huh? You hungry?"

Max was hungry. But, he felt he couldn't give Melvin or anyone else there the idea that he wanted to be there.

"Where am I?" he asked, not looking at Melvin or answering his question.

"Oooh, I think you know where you are," Melvin said, pulling the tray up to the bed, and taking a seat next to where Max still lay. Then he turned to Max. "Now, I suggest we eat while I fill you in on the rules of the games we play here."

Max sat up, placed several pillows behind him, and pulled a sheet over his nakedness.

"You are hungry," Melvin said. "Good."

At first, they ate in silence to satisfy their hunger. But the video was still playing on the television, and Melvin made no move to turn it off. Max ate and listened and refused to look at the television or Melvin. However, the more satiated he became, the less able he was to control what was happening to him underneath the sheet from just listening to the video. He knew Melvin was the one taking him on the video now.

Melvin ate while looking and listening to the television, and occasionally at Max. What was happening on the television made him put his hand on Max's covered thigh, and the more satiated he became, the harder he rubbed it. So, when their hunger for food was satisfied, the hunger in both their groins was causing them to want another kind of satiation.

Melvin was rubbing Max's thigh vigorously, and both of them were breathing hard. He looked at Max as if searching for a sign. Max still refused to look at him, or acknowledge his hand. But his breathing and the bulge beneath his sheet was all Melvin needed to see. Without saying a word, he pushed the cart away and threw back the sheet. Seeing Max's hardening cock with the cock-ring still around it, for an instant they stared into each other's eyes. Then, Melvin suddenly and quickly tightened the ring.

Max closed his eyes and moaned.

As soon as it was tight, taking him by his upper-arm, Melvin slung Max over onto this belly, and was in him before he knew it!

18

At first, Melvin's thrusts were fast and furious, until he was deep inside Max, and his balls were slapping up against Max's ass with each thrust. Now, his thrusts came slower, measured. He brought Max up onto his knees and held his buns apart so that the overhead camera and he could see himself going in deep. Then, pulling out slowly, again and again, as Max, sighing and moaning, took every thrust.

Laying there taking him, Max felt a pleasure like none he'd never experienced. It was the unbound pleasure of submitting to the act. He told himself there had been something in the food. He told himself he could do nothing about what would happen to him here. He thought he had caught a glimpse of Sharon in the video, and he thought about what she had told him, "*It's a way to make some money, so you may as well enjoy it.*" And, despite himself, his moans and sighs made it clear, he did.

Melvin was loudly grunting his pleasure too, with each deep penetrating thrust. And when he thrust himself into Max to the hilt, he came.

Suddenly Max felt his innards go all hot and quivery. It was an anguished exquisite feeling. He sighed, "Let ... me ... cum.... Please ... let me...."

Melvin pulled out and fell on his back. His hard, meaty cock was still standing straight up. Melvin loosened the cock-ring with one hand and pumped Max's cock hard for a few seconds until Max cried out.

He and the overhead camera watched as cum shot from Max, landing hot on his chiseled stomach and on Melvin's resting hand.

Rubbing it into Max's belly and chest and tits, Melvin asked, "Ever heard of dungeons, sweet-ass baby?"

* * * *

Naked, Max sat still letting Melvin, who had donned his robe, bind his wrists. He stood as Melvin took the leather strap up and fastened it around his neck. He was thinking about what Melvin had told him about the rules of the games. He had seen *Eyes Wide Shut*, and somehow he now knew this would get pretty heady. He had to play the game to the end if he wanted their discretion, and money. He sat back on the bed, keeping his gaze straight ahead as Melvin secured the leather straps to each ankle.

Doing this, Melvin had been quiet. "On your knees," he now ordered.

Max complied.

"Lean over onto the bed."

Again, Max complied. He felt Melvin loosen the neck brace, then fasten it back even tighter. He felt the leather go down his back, then around his waist, and he felt straps go around each of his thighs. Then, he felt the leather, greased, thick cock entering him.

Gasping, he felt Melvin slowly pushing the dildo in all the way until he felt his anus muscle close around Melvin's fingers and the leather straps that secured it. One strap led up to the neck brace and two on either side of his balls and cock led to the front of the waistband.

Melvin had said, "*Whenever you're taken out of this room, this is how it'll be.*"

Melvin pulled Max up to his feet, and his head went back to loosen the movement of his wedged-in, leather cock.

"Keep your ass tight … and try not to breathe so hard, baby" Melvin said, taking hold of the loose end of the strap coming from his bound wrists. "You'll push it out, and there's punishment for that," Melvin added, casually.

Then he went to the food cart he had pushed away, and returned to Max with a full glass.

"This will make it all better," he said. "You know, in the real world, I'm a RN."

Holding the glass to Max's mouth, he forced the liquid down his throat. Immediately, Max felt his head swoon.

Melvin had said, "*... And, you are never to say a word... not a word... to anyone.*"

Max's head was swooning, and his anus was burning from its leather tormentor, as Melvin led him down an elegantly appointed hall through a sterile white corridor, and into what looked like a hospital room.

"We'll take it from here," a man in an orderly's uniform said. Melvin dropped the strap, and left Max standing there.

He felt as if he would have fallen had not the two bald, muscled men he noticed just then, taken hold of each arms. Following who Max assumed was a doctor, they brought him to a stainless table in one corner of the large room. The doctor drew the curtains, as the muscle men placed him on the table, face down.

20

Unsure of what was about to happen to him, Max's breathing was coming in fast, short gasps now. He felt the straps being loosened and removed. Slowly, he felt his leather tormentor being pulled out. He was panting hard. The room was spinning. Soon, he felt a hose being guided into him where the tormentor had been. And then the water, warm and soothing, and flushing everything out of him. Afterwards, he was showered off and turned over. He felt the razors on his body, calmly, softly going all over until he was certain the only hair left was on his head. The doctor swabbed both his mouth and the mouth of his penis, and drew four vials of blood. Then the muscle men took his smooth, naked body from the table into the bathroom and into a whirlpool bath of swirling warm water.

* * * *

"How do you want it?!" Max would ask Sharon after the first time she had let him take her from behind.

"In my ass, baby... fuck me in my ass, Big Daddy!" she always cried.

"Beg for it!" he had demanded. *"I want to hear you beg for it. Beg for it!"* he ordered, giving her ass a couple of pops to egg her on.

"Pleassseeee, Big Daddy, pleaseee, fuck me in my ass," she had cried.

And, now he was taking her the way she had asked, as the fire roared! They were both on their knees on the floor in front of the fireplace. He could feel her pushing back onto him as he pushed deeper into her anus. He was experiencing the excitement and gratitude he felt during those first days whenever she had let him take her that way, knowing Kimberly would never allow him to do it that way with her—and knowing there was no need to worry about getting Sharon pregnant.

"Give it to me... Big Daddy! Aahhhhh! You fuck me in my ass, Big Daddy!" he could hear her moaning. *"Aahhhhh... I want to fuck you, Big Daddy. Fuck me... I want to fuck you in your ass, Big Daddy! Fuck me...."* She pushed back rigidly hard and held her breathe while he came, moaning deeply and laying up on her back, still in her.

It was the first time anyone had ever said they wanted to fuck him—much less, in the passions of fucking. And even then he wondered had he cum because he had heard her say it, or because of the pressure she had put on his cock.

"Aahhhhhh," now, it was himself he heard moaning deeply, as if he was off some place far away. His nipples were being nibbled and sucked. "Whooaaaa.... Aahhhh," he moaned as he felt the wet, hot mouths engulf his hard cock and his balls. He was totally aroused and awake. His wrists were again bound and tied to the headboard. He realized he was being taken again.

There were four of them this time, licking, nibbling, sucking and squeezing wherever they touched. All while the television was blaring another of his videos, so that his sighs and moans again echoed throughout room.

"Put the clamps on his nipples!" It was a voice he hadn't heard before. He strained to see who it came from.

"Oohhhhhh!" he cried, and fell back in agony, turning his head from side to side as the pain from the metal clamps being clamped onto each nipple registered.

"He's hard, now tighten him up! Make it good and tight," the voice ordered, and was immediately obeyed.

"Oohhhhh! God!" Max moaned.

"Got nothing to do with it," the voice said in his ear.

Max saw him for the first time when he placed a large, wedged pillow on the bed beside him. His black robe was loose, and Max could see his huge, hard cock with a clear drop of fluid hanging from its tip. To Max it appeared bigger than Melvin's even in both length and width. And its owner, seeing Max looking at it, removed his robe proudly and stood there for an instant, giving him the full view.

"Now, turn his ass over. Get those knees up and hold'em," he ordered.

Face down on the wedged pillow, Max felt the pain from the teeth of the nipple clamps gnawing into him, and it shot an erotic spear through him that made his eyes roll back in their sockets as he swooned in ecstatic agony. Through this, he could feel this new master situating himself between his legs, behind him.

"My johnson's ready to taste some of this sweet meat," he said, slapping Max's buns. Then, he spread them open and massaged his soft, puckered asshole with his thumbs. Instantly, with one plunging push, he rammed his huge hard cock into Max as far as it would go.

"Oohhhhhh…aahhhhh!" Max's cries came from the pain and the ecstasy. He felt like he was being deliciously torn apart. And the pushing sent him forward painfully onto the biting nipple clamps. "Ooohhhhhhh…aaahhhhhhh!" he cried when the huge cock plunged into him even deeper the second time.

"Mmmmm… tight ass, baby! Real hot.. and.. tight!"

Over 7 inches of his rock hard cock was planted in Max's anus, and his new master seemed determined to get the next 4 inches into him. On his knees, using undulating motions, he used his rod to massage the muscles deep within Max, who lay moaning helplessly submitting.

"You want all of this, baby?" he said. "You want 11 inches?! Tell me you want all this cock!" he demanded.

But instead of waiting for a response, he rammed his cock in at least 2 more inches.

"Whooaaaa…. Oohhhhhh! God! Oohhhh Gooddd!" Max cried, "It's too big! Pleaseeee… it hurts!.... It hurt!"

"Damn right, baby!" his master replied, slapping his ass hard and sharp, and ramming himself all the way into Max in one fell swoop. "Damn right!" he shouted, and began wildly pumping his hot hard rod in and out of him, looking a lot like he was riding a horse—fast!

"Ooohhhhhhh! Uuhhhh! Aaahhhhhhhh!" Max's cries and moans came from the pain of the nipple camps, and from the thrusting he was receiving.

"I'm gonna bust your ass wide open tonight!" his tormenting master said. "This good… tight… sweet… ass! Make my dick… feel… so… fucking… good!" he added as he pumped him.

He was enjoying Max, and he was enjoying taking Max for the cameras. He plunged in and pulled out of him for another 10 minutes. Then, ramming himself in as deep as he could go, he threw his arms around Max's thighs and holding his buns tight against him, his first juices shot into him like fire-hot spears.

"Whooaaaaa…. Uh… uh… uh…." he moaned. "Good ass, baby!" he said, patting Max's butt, and quickly pulling out so that the camera could zoom in up close to catch his last cum oozing out.

Max felt his fire-hot cum filling him, and he wanted relief, himself. But he heard Melvin's voice say, *"A slave never asks to cum, unless his master tells him to."* So he lay there, sighing and moaning softly, knowing there would be no soon relief, knowing there would be more to come, when he was turned over onto his back and the wedged pillow was removed.

"Bring me a drink… and take the clamps off," his master ordered from the bed beside him. He was naked, with his back propped on pillows against the headboard. Even limp, the cock that minutes ago had been pounding him seemed huge to Max, as it lay across his tormentor's thigh, pointing toward Max's face.

"Aahhhh! Oohhh!" Max cried as the nipple clamps were removed and immediately he felt the painful pounding of blood rushing through his nipples once more.

"Want a drink, baby?" his master asked. Max didn't—couldn't—reply. "I've got a special drink for you." His new master received his own drink, took a swallow, then, lit a cigarette. "Bring his drink," he ordered.

Soon, Max saw a drink with a bent straw in it being handed to his master, who held his head up and put the straw to his mouth. He held the drink for Max until the glass was empty and Max's head fell back to the bed. He lay there smelling the sweat from their bodies and the smoke from his master's cigarette, hoping something special, something extra, had been placed in his drink. Waiting and wanting it to take affect, because he knew his new master was not finished with him, yet.

* * * *

Now, it was Max taking Kimberly's forearm and turning her over onto her belly. She was breathing hard, anxiously waiting for his penetration, doggy-style, like she had let him do to her before. But suddenly, it was not her vagina he was about to enter!

Quickly she squirmed away from him. Covering herself, she lay looking at him in disgust.

"What are you doing?!"

"I don't want another kid, Kim," Max had protested, falling back on the pillows.

"And I don't want it that way. That's disgusting! That's not the way you're supposed to make love, Max!" Kimberly had cried, as she left the bed, went into the bathroom and closed the door.

Max lay there staring up at the ceiling. Any desire he had had for her that night was gone.

24

Max lay in a stifling, sleepy haze. He had fleeting memories of what had taken place—the new master, a hose, the cleansing. But he had loss all sense of time. And now he realized he was tasting his master's hard, hot cock!

Max's wrists were still bound and tied, his head was spinning, and he was gagging.

Only seconds ago, in his mind, he was in his bedroom with Kimberly. Now, he felt the weight of his master atop his sore nipples, holding his head with both hands and forcing his hard cock down his throat. It was the first time he had ever taken a cock in his mouth, and though he couldn't stop himself from gagging, to his amazement, he didn't find the taste disagreeable.

"Suck it!" his master demanded.

Instantly, he closed his mouth onto the huge cock and began sucking it like he had never been able to do to a woman. And suddenly realizing his cock was being sucked too, made him pull on his master's gland, gluttonously.

"Aaahhhhh, baby! Your ass feels so damn good!" his master cried.

Once again the heat consumed him. He was enjoying the feel and the sound of the hard, hot cock thrusting in and out of his mouth, and the hot, wet mouth consuming his own. When, suddenly his master's hand withdrew his throbbing rod and hot, thick cum covered Max's face and neck.

When Max felt the cum rushing through him, he didn't realize he was no longer wearing the cock-ring until he felt it shoot into the mouth and onto the face of the one who had been sucking him.

Some time after that performance, Max opened his eyes to find himself back in his room with Melvin, his guide and secretly the one he loved to make love to him most.

"A good fuck really knocks your ass right on out, don't it nigga?" Melvin said, lying naked next to Max on the bed with the remote in his hand. He turned his attention back to the television that was showing yet another video of him and his latest tormentor.

"They want to hear you cry out and moan more, baby, like you just did. You see, all these fuckas got some big-ass dicks. And they want to know you're feeling it when they put it to your ass. You understand?" Melvin asked as he got up to turn the television off and put the remote away.

Max didn't reply, but lay there staring at Melvin's nakedness. He couldn't believe he had taken all of him.

Not hearing a response, Melvin turned and quickly came back to the bed. The open-handed slap struck Max's jaw so hard, it blinded him for an instant before he realized Melvin had hit him!

"You understand?!" Melvin insisted.

Max's first instinct was to hit him back. But he remembered the situation he was in–he had no idea where he was, he had been taken in one way or another almost continually since he had been there, and from the way he was feeling he realized Melvin had probably just fucked him even in his sleep—and now he was feeling the sting of Melvin's open-handed slap. He couldn't believe he had gotten himself into this situation. Yet, as all these things passed through his mind, he realized he had.

Rubbing his jaw, he simply said, "I understand, man!"

"This is serious business here," Melvin said, relenting and rubbing Max's thigh. "It's all about big dicks, big money, and these guys don't play! I brought you here, so I'm responsible for your ass ... and you're gonna do me proud." Now, he crawled onto the bed on his knees straddling Max. "Tomorrow, I'm taking you to the gym...." he was saying. "They want to see you perform there."

The bout of anger seemed to have settled in Melvin's cock. It was sticking straight out as Melvin crawled up to Max's chest.

"Now, I'm gonna show you how to suck a cock!" he said.

* * * *

The next morning, Max was surprised when Melvin escorted him to the gym without the tormenting paraphernalia he had put on—and in—him before. They each wore only a jock-strap underneath their sweatpants, and jackets.

Max was able to see just how beautiful the Lodge was. On their way to the gym, they passed by an elegantly furnished dining room where two people, a black man and a white man, sat at one of the tables quietly talking to each other. Max

26

thought the black guy looked somewhat familiar. But, if they noticed Max and Melvin at all, neither acknowledged them. Through the windows of another well appointed room, Max caught a glimpse of a manicured lawn that went on as far as he could see. But he could see nothing to give him a hint of where he was.

Arriving at a gym large enough to have several pieces of the latest exercise equipment on the market, Max counted six other guys working out. Four were working alone, two were working together. They were all wearing only jock-straps, and though Max had been warned not to look at anyone too closely, he couldn't help noticing the bulges they barely concealed.

First, Melvin took Max to the locker room where they removed their sweats. Then, he guided him to the weighs, and slant-board. Now, the two who were working out together gave heads-up to Melvin, and Max felt them giving him greedy looks.

Melvin and Max had been working out long enough for sweat to be pouring from both of them, as Max lay on the slant-board on his back, lifting 20 pound weights in each hand. He was holding them up long enough for Melvin to add 5 more pounds to each weight before he realized the room had emptied, save for one of the two who had been working together.

Now, he joined them.

"Turn him over, Mel," he ordered. "Let's see if he can lift this," he said, cupping his crouch, "if he's on his belly."

Max could see that he was pulling off his jock-strap while Melvin took the weighs and did as he was ordered to do. Then, when he was on his stomach on the slant-board, between his legs, this new master leaned over him and straightened out his arms. Melvin placed a 15 pound weight in each hand.

"Now, lift them," he ordered, bringing his own hands slowly down Max's back to his buns, where they massaged for a while. "Uummm... beautiful... meaty.... Did you oil him up?" Max heard his new master ask Melvin, who was on his knees in front of Max. Max could see Melvin's bulge growing bigger.

"He's fuckin' ready," Melvin assured him.

And suddenly Max felt his new master's hands on his sides as they grasped the jock-strap he was wearing, and slowly sled it down pass his knees, and off, as he struggled with lifting the weights.

"Keep lifting," he ordered Max, as he forced each of his legs over the slant-board handles so that his penis and balls hung down, freely. Situating himself at Max's ass, so that his huge rod was ready to enter, he took Max's cock in his left hand, his own in his right.

Now, Max could no longer lift the weights. His new master was hand-pumping them both, simultaneously, until his own huge cock hung engorged to the max. Then, putting it once again to Max, he forced it all the way into the oil-rich, waiting hole in three powerful plunges.

"Uuhhh! Uuhhhh! Uuhhhhh!" Max cried at each one. "Oooohhhh! Aaaahhhhh!" he moaned when all 12 inches were inside him.

"Man!" his new master cried, "This shit's good, mane! Tight! Hot.... Fuck!"

Max lay with his arms straight out, his hands tightly clutching the weights.

His new master was balancing himself with both hands grasping Max's lower back and hips, as he began rhythmically thrusting his huge cock in and out of him.

"Let him eat you!" he ordered Melvin, breathlessly, as he continued pumping Max. "I want to see him sucking your dick!"

On his knees in front of Max, Melvin's cock was already hard. Now, he sent it into Max's gasping mouth.

"Take it, baby! Take it like I showed you! Aaaahhhh!" he sighed, as Max's lips clamped down tight onto him. Max's sucking was soon in tune with his new master's thrusts.

"Damn! This ass is good, mane! Suck it!" his master ordered, and slapped his ass!

"Aaaahhhhh... suck it, baby! Take it down you throat! Suck it!" Melvin cried.

"Mmmmm! Mmmm!" Max gasped. He could hardly breathe. Taking it from both ends he felt like he was in a movie—and he was. He knew he wanted to satisfy Melvin. And, for the first time since he arrived there, as it was happening, he realized he was enjoying the feel of a real, big, hard cock.

"Aaaahhhhh! Aaaahhhhh!" Melvin moaned. Taking hold of Max's head, he was forcing him down onto his steaming rod, even as the master continued thrusting his massive cock in and out of him. "Whoooaaa ... I'm gonna cum! Whoooaaa, baby! I'm gonna cum!" Melvin cried, as cum shot from him, down Max's gagging throat and out his mouth and nose.

Then, still on his knees, Melvin fell back onto his legs, his spent cock limply dangling in front of Max's wet face.

"You whiz," the new master chided Melvin, while holding his hard, throbbing cock deep within Max's pulsating anus. "Leave us! This is mines, now!"

And with that, he continued his deep, penetrating, machine-like pumping, as the camera caught the full action, up close, from the rear.

Soon his master's deep penetrations became longer and longer, Max knew he would soon blow.

"Whooaa! This is good, baby! Your ass's gooood!" he cried, as the thick, hot cum shot from this master's cock, spilling onto Max's wet, steaming ass.

He tried to withdraw for the camera. Coming out just enough for the camera to see, he plummeted back into Max's seething, hot, bottom, and lay atop his back with it planted there, moaning: "Uuhhh! Uuhhh! Uuhhh!" until the camera went black.

Finally, his new master pulled out. Forcibly sitting Max up, he took a bottle of water, shook it, opened it and gave it to him.

"Drink it," he said. "You're going to need it."

Max turned the bottle up and drank every drop. He couldn't tell whether it was his need for water or what was in it that made him feel so good.

Taking Max's arm, and helping him up, his master said, "Come on, baby. You're still on. Guests are waiting to meet you in the sauna."

When they entered the steaming room, Max saw that everyone who had been in the gym when he and Melvin first arrived, was now in the sauna. Through the steam, he could see them all seated on the benches with their towels draped over them, like they were in a roman bath. The floor of the round room was matted with a drain in the center of the mat. Max watched his master place the slant-board in the center of the mat, over the drain. He knew what was to come.

His master then came to him and fell to his knees. Taking Max's dripping cock in his hands, he put the cock-ring on, bringing his balls up into it. Breathing hard, Max closed his eyes, and his head rolled back as his master did this. Next, his master laid him on his belly on the slant-board, placing his legs outside the handles, like before. Then he situated himself on his knees in front of Max, like Melvin had done before.

"Number one!" he called, and the first one stood, dropped his towel, and stepped down from the benches.

Momentarily, Max felt him enter his oiled, cum-filled anus. He, like all the others, was as big as his master. And as he, and all the others, took turns plunging in and out of him over and over again and again, his master's cock was also wearing a cock-ring, and was in his mouth the whole while.

While taking them all, whatever was in the water had him teetering on the edge of consciousness. He had no idea how long they had ran the train on him. But, at some point he found himself seated on cool marble in the shower with cooling water sprinkling down on him. Slowly, coming around, he realized his master was bathing him. He was still wearing the cock-ring. On the floor, in front of him with the water coming down, his master now took his hard, aching rod into his mouth, and holding it deep down his throat, he removed the cock-ring. Max sighed erotically each time he felt his cum escape in small, prolonged explosions, because the swallowing muscles in his master's throat was at the head of his cock, and stopped each cum-filled explosive mouthful every time he swallowed it down.

He didn't know when it started, but to Max everything had now began to seem and feel like being in a dream. He soon lost count of how many men had had him, and he had no idea of how many more were to come. He still could not admit to himself that he had come to this place knowingly, willingly, perhaps even wanting what was happening to him. He still could not fully admit to himself that something in him was enjoying the helplessness of the situation he found himself in, that he was enjoying the feel of a hard, throbbing cock in him, and that he wanted to be taken that way. He found himself willingly taking every drug they gave him so he could lose himself in the dream of it all. That way, he could give in to it, and feel and enjoy the pleasure of it, without feeling the guilt of wanting what all his life he had been taught, was a sin.

Chapter III

He had lost count of how many days he had been there. And it no longer mattered to him who his master was to be. He no longer looked at them. He just felt them as they kept coming and coming and coming. Soon the day came when he realized something was different. He had been allowed to sleep late, alone. He was awakened as the waiter he had seen on his first day there wheeled a cart into the room. Then, almost as soon as Max had eaten his fill of the meal, mostly peeled fruits and vegetables, the waiter reappeared and removed the tray. Then, just as suddenly, Melvin entered the room and started taking off his clothes.

"What time is it?" he asked.

"It doesn't matter," Melvin responded. Handing him a pill and a glass of water, he added, "Take this. I've got to get you ready."

Max sat up and took the water looking at Melvin. Like an obedient patient, he opened his mouth to let Melvin place the pill on his tongue, then he swallowed it. Max watched in silence as Melvin pulled out a suitcase from underneath the bed. Peering into it, Max saw that it contained all the paraphernalia and the tormentor Melvin had used to dress him on that first day. Only this tormentor was bigger, longer and thicker than the first one. And there was a mask, a black mask glistening with rhinestones all along the edge.

"Get up!" Melvin ordered, and Max complied. "In here," he led him into the bathroom. Melvin turned the water on in the tub. "Get in and get on your knees," he ordered.

Max complied. With his backside to the running water, seconds passed and he sighed as he felt the cold nozzle enter. He arched his back up as he felt his bowels fill. On bent knees, Melvin held him back on his legs. He grunted as his bowels emptied.

"Again," Melvin said, and Max was again back on all four with the nozzle filling him, until again he was held back and emptied once more.

"One more time," Melvin said, and the process was repeated.

Now, Max had been purged several times since he had been there. But never three times in a row!

Next, Max heard and felt the buzz of the razor, as Melvin shaved him.

Then, cleansing Max and the tub, Melvin let it fill with warm water and gently bathed his charge, who lay back with his eyes closed, empty, exhausted and swooning from the ordeal and the pill.

When he was done, Melvin stood Max up to dry him. Max felt shaky. He hadn't questioned Melvin about the pill, but he knew it was taking affect.

Leaning him against the wall, Melvin started drying his shoulders, working his way down his dark back first, then his buns. He parted them, dried them; then he rimmed his anus for as long as he dared, as Max moaned his pleasure and arched his butt to receive it. Melvin kept drying. Turning him around and coming back up his legs, his mouth grasped Max's ready, hard cock that was pointing straight at him.

"Good," Melvin said as his mouth grasped it and he sucked hard, pushing Max's buns back against the wall. Then he gave him another hard, pulling suck that forced Max's pelvis back out, as he came up off of it.

"Aahhhh!" Max moaned, as his freed cock bounced a couple of times. Then Melvin continued drying him off.

"They want you hard, baby," he said, placing a cock-ring on Max's hungry rod, and tightening it. Then he took him back into the bedroom.

"On your knees ... bend over," he ordered. Max knew what was coming first this time.

On his knees, bent across the bed, Max felt the syringe enter his anus. He could feel the soothing oil being pumped in. And when it was withdrawn, he felt the tormentor. From what he had seen, he knew he had to be taking over 10 inches of rock-hard leather.

"Uh! Uh! Uuhhh!" he groaned, as Melvin forced the dildo inside him.

When it disappeared inside and his rectal muscle closed round Melvin's fingers, he drew two of the three straps that were hanging from it up in front of Max on either side of his cock and balls, and fastened them to a strap around his waist. Then he brought them on up over his shoulders, and down to the back of the waist strap. Next he brought the third strap tightly up between his buns and connected it to the waist strap.

"There. Hold it tight, baby," he said, standing him up and looking him over.

Satisfied with his work, he sat on the bed and took another long, leather lariat from the suitcase. With it he slowly, meticulously bound Max's wrists, and tied a noose on the other end and laid it across the bed. Now he went to the closet

32

and returned with two, long robes, a black one and a white one. He threw the black one around his shoulders, fastened it, and donned one of the masks. Then he draped the white robe over Max's shoulders, and carefully placed the white mask on him.

"This is it, baby!" he said, giving Max another pill and holding the cocktail chaser to his mouth until the glass was empty. "This is why I brought your ass here," he whispered into Max's ear.

He grabbed the noose on the end of the lariat, and guided Max out.

Everyone in the room wore masks or had their faces made up in a manner that reminded Max of a bacchanal he had seen once in a movie. He sensed he was to be the main course of this feast. Some of the masks were elaborately decorated. Others were plain. All wore robes. Though they all stood around the grand room in small groups. Max could hear only dream-like silence and see only laughter from peering, piercing eyes.

Once they entered the center of the room, Melvin removed Max's robe and placed it over his arm. Slowly, he led Max around the entire room, as all the others turned peering at him through their painted and mask-covered faces as he passed. Somehow, he realized, they were all men.

After Melvin had led him around the room a couple of times, he was led out. The music started, and the robed men standing in small groups began drinking and talking to each other in murmurs. Max felt as if he was moving in slow motion, though only moments passed as Melvin guided him to the back of the stage. With a drum roll, those in the room gathered around the stage, and Melvin led Max out onto it. He stood him in front of a padded, velvet covered slant-board. The drum roll continued, and Max heard someone call out the first number over a microphone.

"Number 5!" the voice rang.

Immediately one of the robed, masked men came out of the audience onto the stage, holding up a chip with the number 5 on it. He said nothing.

Dropping his robe, he revealed a throbbing, hard cock. He gave Melvin the chip, and Melvin gave him Max's leash. Bringing Max around to the high side of the slant-board, he turned him so that his rear was to the audience, and laid him face down on it. On his knees, off to the side so that everyone could see, he untied his captive's harness, and slowly withdrew the leather tormentor.

"Aaaahhhhhh," Max sighed, automatically, in relief.

Applause rang out from the audience.

Now, number 5 stood over Max parting his buns to reveal his seething, oil-filled anus to all who could see. Lowering himself he moved his hands to Max's back for balance, he plunged his cock into his captive's waiting, oil-oozing cavity.

"Huhhh! Aaaahhhhhh!" the automatic sigh was pushed from Max's throat once more.

"Mmmmm!" moaned number 5. And now, the show was on!!

A bright spotlight kept the action on the stage clearly visible to anyone who cared to watch. A simulcast recording of it could be seen even larger than life from two large overhead screens for any who wanted to watch close up. Many did. But soon some paired off and disappeared into side rooms. And though the audience was having fun, laughing and talking with each other, the overriding sounds that filled the grand room were the cries, sighs and moans coming from Max and number 5. Then, Max and number 4. Next, Max and number 3, Max and number 2, and finally, the number 1 was called.

The last pill and cocktail Melvin had given him, and the four poundings he had taken, left Max laying there erotically exhausted, limp and dazed. The only thing he could hear was his own heavy breathing. The only thing he could feel was a sweet, throbbing ache. But now number 1, the masked Soledad, stood over him.

Many in the audience crowded around the stage when the number was called, anxious to view his famous, 13" cock. Again, applause rang out when Soledad's robe was removed. It appeared to have a life of its own—pulsating, hanging there stiffly, as if being held up by an invisible thread, it was well pass half the length of his thigh, and it had to be at least 6 inches in diameter! And in one powerful thrust, he plunged the fully-engorged head and nearly 6 inches of it into Max's seething ass!

"Huuhhhhh!! .. Oooohhhhh!" Max cried, loudly, as sweat and tears poured from him. "Whooooaaahhh!"

Wild applause came from the audience.

Another powerful thrust, another 3 inches!

"Ooohhhhh! Whooaaa!" Max cried, breathlessly, hearing only louder applause from their audience.

Max moaned and cried out again and again, until just about all 13" of Soledad's cock disappeared into him. And he could still hear applause as Soledad pressed, and held his huge cock deep within him for what to him seemed like forever. Soledad leaned over onto his back and through his mask, he breathlessly whispered in Max's ear:

"It's good, baby.... Hot!! Mmmmm..." Soledad breathed through his teeth. "You got a mutha-fuckin' sweet ass, baby! And it's taking it all!!"

With that, he began with slow, powerful plunges, pulling out to the head, then plunging in as deep as he could go, and holding it. With his eyes closed, engrossed in the feeling, slowly Soledad's body went into rhythmic thrusts that could only be described as machine-like—automatic! His breath and his sighs were almost inaudible.

But Max's sensuous moans and cries were loud and deep. He had no idea where he was, what time it was, nor how long he had been on the slant-board. All he knew was that all the times he had been taken before paled in comparison to what he was taking now from Soledad. Each plunge elicited an exquisitely painful, guttural moan.

Deep within him, Max felt a pain like none he had ever known. It was the sweet, agonizing pain he felt he had to pay for willingly letting men do to him what all his life he had been taught a sin. But for Max it was an exquisitely erotic pain. He could feel the head of Soledad's humongous cock stirring a place so deep within him, he never knew it existed. With tears and sweat pouring from him, Max could barely think. His entire body was on fire, as his mind and body endured what he experienced as a deliciously erotic pleasure and the pain....

"Seventy-seven ... seventy-eight ... seventy-nine ... eighty...." Max's consciousness somehow heard the audience chanting. He realized they were counting as Soledad came out, then plunged his huge member ever deeper into him, holding it in longer and longer. And they counted.

"Eighty-seven.... Eighty-eight.... Eighty-nine.... Ninety!"

Sweating and crying, even craving the erotic pain and pleasure of it despite himself, Max did and didn't want it to stop.

But now, with each plunge into this giving anus, Soledad was feeling his urge mounting.

"One hundred one.... One hundred two.... One hundred three.... One hundred four.... One hundred five...."

Now Soledad's plunges were so deep his balls bulged as his meat disappeared into Max, and he held himself there.

"One hundred seven! One hundred eight! One hundred nine! One hundred ten! Aaaaahhhhhh!" the audience roared as Soledad pulled out quickly and his cum spattered all over Max's ass. Then he sent his still massive, cumming cock back into the glistening tunnel once more.

Panting, he laid himself up on Max's back.

"It's the sweetest... hottest... ass-pussy, I ever had, baby!!" he said between urgent gasps. "Oooohhhhh! ..." as cum shot from him. "A real hot!... sweet ass!"

Chapter IV

The summer sun was bearing down hard on the field, so Max stood in the dugout watching practice when Donnie Williams and his son, Trey, came up to him.

"Dad, this is Brian's dad," Trey said, introducing his dad to Max. "Tell 'em what you said about Brian," Trey called, running out onto the file to join his team.

"Hey man," Donnie said, offering Max his hand. "Me and my son think your boy's the best hitter they've got here."

"I think we've both got a couple of heavy hitters on our hands," Max said, while shaking his hand. "I'm Max.... You—you look familiar! ... I remember! You used to play for...."

"That was ages ago, man," Donnie cut him off. "Now, I'm just a regular businessman ... always keeping my eye out for new talent, though."

Max was happy and proud that Donnie Williams, the former big-time major leaguer, was saying this to him about his son. Somewhere in the back of his mind he thought that maybe what he went through to get his son into this private training camp might have been worth it.

"I've watched Trey hit. He's got a lot of power," Max said.

"Yeah, this is his third year here. He's good, but I've watched your boy. Now he can go all the way! He's a natural."

"Well, I'm hoping," he said proudly.

After hearing Donnie Williams say his son was a natural, Max didn't hear much of anything else. So the two men stood there, saying very little, watching their sons practice.

Max's mind was on where it had been ever since he left. His son had been in the camp for two weeks, and now he had validation from someone he knew had connections. For the first time since he returned from the Lodge there was no doubt in his mind that getting his son into this training camp was worth it.

* * * *

The aroma of cooking bacon wafting into the room had awakened Max that morning, now over four weeks ago. He had come to drowsily on Sharon's bed. He had no idea how he had gotten there. For an instant he wondered if it all had been a dream. He was naked and his whole body felt used. When he first sat up he felt woozy, but otherwise he felt fine. That morning, thinking about all he had been through—all they had done to him, he didn't know how he felt about anything anymore.

The clothes and the shoes he had worn to Sharon's house five days before now lay neatly across a chair. He smelled bacon and eggs, and he realized he was hungry. He quickly showered and dressed and went into the kitchen where he found Sharon cooking, alone.

"Darling!" she called, "Hello! Come in, have a seat, and count your money! I'm making you breakfast."

Max went to the table and sat down, picked up the stack of money, and started counting.

"How long have I been here?"

"Oh, several hours," Sharon said, coming to the table with a plate of bacon and another with a stack of pancakes. "Want eggs?" she asked.

"No."

He didn't know how he felt about Sharon anymore, either.

When they first met he was sure she was the one for him. He had found her fine, beautiful, intelligent, carefree and easy. Just the opposite of Kimberly, he thought. It had been some of the best sex he had ever had. And when she used the strap-on on him—that first time—he had found it undeniably the most thrilling feeling he had ever experienced. What he wanted sexually, he had gotten from her. What he felt for her, he would realize, had been pure, unadulterated lust for her body, and for the new sex she had introduced him to.

Max had counted out $10,000.00 and put it in his pocket before he began eating. Sharon sensed his mood and realized he didn't want to talk. She quietly laid his car keys on the table beside his plate. Then, she sat down and they ate in silence.

When he finished, he stood up.

"I'm done with it. Don't call me again, Sharon, and I won't call you," he said, simply, taking his keys.

"If that's how you want it, darling," Sharon said, without the least bit of infliction in her voice.

Max couldn't tell how she felt about him or what he said. He was heading for the door.

"You should know, though…" Sharon said, "… it's out of my control…. And I'm keeping the poems."

Max stopped, and turned to her. He hadn't thought about his writing, his poems, for some time now.

"I'm keeping them," Sharon said, coming to him. "All … except this one. You wrote it… oh, about a month ago" she said, handing him a folded piece of paper.

Max opened it, and Sharon looked on as he silently read:

To Sharon

You said, let me do it to you
* And you meant it*
I said, yes
* And I meant it.*

You were like me
Your lips, your tongue,
your hands make me feel sooo good
They part, I'm entered, I cry out in exaltation
I have never felt sooo good!

You asked did I like that
* Do I want more*
I said, yes
* And I mean it.*

Max

"Keep this one too," Max said, handing the paper back to her. "I don't want it."

Then, he left.

"Daddy! Daddy!" Brian called, as he ran into the house ahead of his mother after seeing his dad's car in the garage. "I knew you would be home today! I just knew it!" he said, excitedly hugging Max.

"I'm glad to see you too, son!" Max said, smiling and hugging his boy. "I had to get back here in time for you to start training." He was looking at Kimberly, who had followed their son in. "It's good to see you, too," he said to her. "I missed you."

With that, she too came into his arms.

As he stood there hugging Brian and Kimberly, he decided then and there that he would never see Sharon again. That he would never again do what he had spent the last four days and nights doing. He would do what he needed to do to be a father for Brian, and the man Kimberly wanted him to be, is what he thought.

He felt he had to let his mustache grow back.

* * * *

"I'm opening the gym up every Sunday for the team, while they're in camp," Donnie Williams was saying as the boys were coming off the field. "You and Brian should come over and work out. Hey, bring the family; we have a section and classes for the ladies...."

"Can we, Dad?!" Brian asked, eagerly excited about the invitation.

"You and your mom go to church on Sundays," Max said to him.

"We're open on Sundays 'til 7," Donnie said, "you guys can come after church."

"Okay, maybe we will," Max said. "Thanks for the invite, man," he added, gathering Brian's equipment.

"We're gonna go, ain't we, Dad?!" Brian asked, as they headed for the car. "I mean, Trey said they got all kinds of neat stuff! Like a pool ... inside! And equipment ... and a steam room...."

"Sauna," Max said, crawling in behind the wheel. He couldn't help remembering the last time he was in a sauna. He felt his body grow hot as he drove off.

Unseen and unbeknown to Max, as soon as Donnie S. Williams heard Max say the word "sauna," he propped his leg up on the bench and leaned forward to

40

conceal the huge hard bulging inside his sweats. He and Max had the same pecan-brown complexion, but his tall, lean athletic physique was all muscle, and a bit slimmer. Both he and Max's hair was close-cut, exposing a sea of black, tight waves on his head. And though he and Max were about the same age, he was clean-shaven and it made him look younger than Max.

He had seen Max a couple of times from the distance of his car since that night over four weeks ago when he, as Soledad, had leaned upon his back and whispered, breathlessly, *"You got a sweet ass, baby... Hot! Sweet ass!"*

But Max had been on his mind every since that night! And Sharon had promised him, he would have him. She had a plan, and now they were working it.

Now, this was the first time he had seen Max up close, in regular clothes, and it was the first time they had spoken. He didn't like the mustache, but just being close enough to him once more that he could touch him and smell a whiff of his sweat had stirred a force within Donnie S. Williams that wouldn't be denied or contained.

"Can I tell coach to bring the team on Sundays?" Trey asked, as Max and Brian drove away.

"Coach already knows, son," Donnie replied. "Com'on, let's go see your mother."

* * * *

Max had grown much more circumspect since experiencing the ordeals that had taken place in his life over the last month. He didn't know what to expect at Donnie's gym, but Coach had said only good things about it, and Brian was adamant about coming.

So, there they were.

"Neat!" Brian said, as he came through the door. "Look at all this equipment! Look Dad!" he said, pointing up.

"That looks like an overhead track," Max explained, looking up at the balcony going clean around the second floor.

"Wow!" Brian exclaimed, as Trey and Donnie came up to greet them.

41

"That's exactly what it is," Donnie said, playfully mauling Brian's head while smiling at Max.

"Glad you could make it, man," he added, extending his hand.

"Well, Brian wouldn't have it no other way," Max said. Taking Donnie's hand, they gave each other the *brotha* handshake.

"I thought you'd bring the Mrs."

"She's got some program at church," Max explained. "Looks like a great place you've got here," he added, looking around.

"Thanks. Ah, Trey, why don't you show Brian and his dad ... Max, right?" Donnie feigned.

"Right," Max said.

"Why don't you show them around? I've got a couple of things I've got to check on in the office." Extending his hand to Max who shook it, he added: "See you around, man. Glad you brought your son."

He headed off before Max could reply.

Alone, in his office, Donnie sat at his desk with a remote in hand. Pointing it to what appeared to be a paneled wall, the wall slid open from the middle revealing a bank of video monitors. Finding Trey, Brian and Max, he followed them as they moved from one piece of equipment to another. He was still following Max on the monitors as he picked up the phone, and dialed.

She answered.

"He's here," Donnie said simply, without averting his eyes from Max on the monitor.

The boys had left him at the weights. Now Max was removing his sweats. Underneath he was wearing black, tight shorts and a matching tank. He lay on a bench on his back with 20 pound weights in each hand, bench pressing them. Using the remote, Donnie was able to zoom in between his legs so he could see the impression his balls made through the tight shorts.

"Darling, we knew he'd come," Sharon said, reassuringly. "Now, if you want that ass, and I know you do, you'd better start thinking of a way to get it. And, believe me, baby, that won't be too hard. He's still fighting it, but he loves the dick, really. He really does!"

After they hung up, Donnie watched Max on every machine he used, and in the sauna. When Max went into the bath to shower, Donnie hurried there. He was standing over a urinal with his huge, 13" cock in his hand when Max came out with a towel tied at his waist. Certain Max had seen him, he smiled, shook it, and casually put it away. Then, he washed his hands.

"Hey bro, get a good workout?!" he asked, nonchalantly.

"Ah … yeah!" Max's reply was measured, trying to contain his own rush of erotic excitement.

"Oh! By the way," Donnie called back as he headed out the door. "Some of the members come over once or twice a week for a little game … not much … just chump change, mostly, on Wednesday nights. You ought to join us! You might win a little … or bring me some luck!"

"Thanks, man," Max replied. "Maybe I will."

Indeed, Max had seen him. And in the seeing, his blood ran hot! He couldn't help himself. He had never seen a bigger cock.

No longer able to control what was suddenly happening to him, he went back into the shower, locked the door and turned on the water. Standing underneath the running water, he sent the fingers on his left hand into his anus, with his right hand grasping his hard, throbbing cock, he pumped it hard and fast until cum shot from him, and splattered onto the wall. Disgusted and humiliated with his inability to contain the urge that had suddenly gripped him, he turned the showerhead to the wall, and watched the water wash his cum down the drain.

He dressed, slowly. He felt confused, and an excitement he hadn't experienced since leaving the Lodge. And Donnie sat in his office, sipping his coconut rum over ice, and watching him all the while. When Max and Brian were ready to leave, Donnie hurried from his office once again in time to catch them at the door.

"Hey," he said to Brian, mostly, "you get a good workout?!"

"Yeah. It was great! I used…."

"Every piece of equipment you got in there," Max said, cutting him off. Suddenly feeling uncomfortable about the feeling seeing Donnie had aroused in him. "It was really great," he said. He felt he had to get away.

"Well, that's why I open it up for you guys. You can come whenever you want to…." Now, he turned to Max. "Like I said, we have a game most Wednesday nights, while the boys are in the gym. You and Brian are welcome to com'on by."

"Yeah, Brian," Trey chimed in. "Coach comes, and he really makes us work out. And then the chef from the restaurant serves us up! It's great!"

"Wow! Can we, Dad?!"

"Let's see whether your mom's got something planned before we commit, son," Max said. "I'll let you know, man," he answered Donnie and really looked at him, for the first time allowing himself to see his dark, strikingly arresting handsomeness.

"Good enough," Donnie said, lightly. "Here, take my card. Just give me a call."

Thinking about Donnie's huge cock, Max thought Donnie had deliberately touched his hand as he gave him the card. Whether Donnie deliberately did or not, his touch had sent a surge throughout Max. It was a surge he wouldn't soon forget.

* * * *

"Hell no, mutha-fucka! You ain't gonna fuck my ass up no more! You know I can't take all that thing in *my* ass!" Pretty Boy said, scurrying away from the bed and Donnie's grasp. Grabbing his pants from a nearby chair and hastily getting into them, he added, "I thought all you wanted was head, anyway!"

"Get the fuck out of here," Donnie shouted. "I don't need your ass!"

"And, I don't need your ass, either! You're not sending me back to the fucking doctor!" he yelled, stuck out his tongue to Donnie, then slammed the door.

Moments before, Pretty Boy had been lusciously licking Donnie, and sucking his balls, as Donnie lie there erotically enjoying the sensations while looking at the video from the lodge of himself, as Soledad, taking Max.

But when the audience began the countdown on the video, Donnie's desire for penetration overtook him. When Pretty Boy realized what he was half-heartedly trying to do, they tussled. Pretty-boy managed to slip from Donnie's grip, and scurry from the bed.

Donnie didn't really want Pretty Boy that way any more, if he ever had. He had been enjoying the pleasures of his hands, mouth, and mostly his tongue, for some time now. But actually Donnie found Pretty Boy too pretty and too flamboyantly feminine for his taste. Yet, he knew Pretty Boy would do just about anything he asked him to do. And he felt that Pretty Boy was really a good friend, and a good person at heart. *"After all…"* Donnie would tell people, *"…he's the only one around here volunteering to work at the AIDS hospice. And, if he can do that— he's braver than me!"* Donnie would add, sincerely.

Sometimes he felt Pretty Boy really did want him to take him again. But the memory of the first and only time he took him, when he had gotten high on a bad trip and had raped him, was still all too vivid in his mind. He had been able to ram almost half of himself into him before he realized Pretty Boy was screaming, and the wetness he felt was blood on his hands.

Blood was the one thing Donnie had never been able to tolerate.

Donnie's doctor had come immediately to treat Pretty Boy, and stitch him up. Donnie had taken care of him ever since, and he vowed to himself that he would never, forcibly, take Pretty Boy again.

Now, Donnie lay there alone in the dark using his own hands. The sound of the video audience counting filled the room and thoughts and visions and feelings of him plunging into Max filled his head.

"One hundred seven! One hundred eight!"

That's what I want! That's what I need!

"One hundred nine! One hundred ten! Aaaaahhhhhh!" the audience roared as Donnie Soledad Williams pulled out, quickly, and his cum spattered all over Max's ass! Then he plunged his cock back deep into the glistening tunnel.

"Mmmmmm," Donnie sighed. Now, his hands were wet with his own juices.

Chapter V

One night late that summer, Max managed to continue cuddling Kimberly as they lay on their sides in bed together. He pulled out of her just before he came. And, after the cum, had come the emptiness that had been slowly consuming him ever since he left the Lodge. It was a deep emptiness that comes with a longing for something more. A longing that he had allowed to consume and satiate his mind only once since then – that Sunday when he saw Donnie's huge phallus, in the shower at the gym. Now, lying beside Kimberly with Donnie filling his head, Max felt confused and frustrated with himself, and totally unable to get to sleep.

I've got to get him out of my mind, he thought. *I've got to keep it out... of... my head!*

"Daddy! Daddy!" Brian called, busting into their room and jumping on the bed with them. "Can I see if Trey can go to Disney World with me and mom?! Can I?! He said he's never been, either! Can I ask him, mama?!" Brian pled.

Max looked to Kimberly, who was sitting up, now. Somehow, Trey going to Disney World with Brian and Kimberly seemed right to him.

"I don't know ... what do you think?" Kimberly asked looking at Max.

"He seems like a good kid," Max replied. "I think he likes this joker here," he said, grabbing Brian and tickling him. "It might be good for Brian to have somebody there... you know, someone his own age. Somebody to hang with."

Giggling, Brian sat up. "Yeah mama, I'm gonna need somebody to hang with... and somebody to go on rides with. You're not gonna wanna ride on everything with me!" Brian declared. "Is she, Dad?"

Max laughed. "I don't think so. I think he's got you there," he said to Kimberly, leaving the bed.

"Well, what about his mom and dad?" she asked. "You think they'll let him go?"

"I haven't met his mom," Max said. "Let me talk to his dad, and we'll see." He left the bed. Grabbing his son from the bed, and playfully holding him by the shoulders, he marches him into the kitchen where he made them cereal. Max was silently thinking, now, I *need* to talk with him!

46

As he sat across the table, eating and listening to his son talk of his plans for Disney World, Max's mind drifted back to where it was before Brian had burst into their bedroom.

He thought it strange, yet somehow wonderful, that Brian had given him what he felt was a legitimate reason to call Donnie, whose image had added to the confusion in his mind ever since he caught site of him that day. He instantly convinced himself that he would never have called Donnie Williams on his own. Yet, since that day, each time he made love to Kimberly, he longed to feel something else. Something in him knew it was Donnie, but he couldn't bring himself to admit that. What he could admit was he wanted the helplessness of the feeling he had felt at the Lodge.

He could hardly wait for Brian and Kimberly to get home from church that Sunday.

* * * *

"Well, thanks man, I was counting on you to bring me luck!" Donnie said, laughingly to Max, while raking in the pot of money on the table.

"Ah man! You just found somebody who don't know yo' bluff!" the guy Donnie had introduced as Perry Rogier, a real estate broker, said. "You're up next, man!" he then said to Max, ".... Will you please give me something?!"

Everyone around the table laughed, as Max took the deck and shuffled.

"I'll try to do you right, man," Max said, dealing.

Donnie left the table, motioning for one of the other two guys waiting to play to take his place.

"That's good! That's good!" Perry Rogier was saying, raking in his cards. Laughter and ribbings came from all around the table.

Max had been apprehensive about joining the game. He remembered reading something about the covers men on the DL used, and he felt certain this could be one of them. So, since he and Brian had been coming to the gym, he hadn't accepted Donnie's invitation. But, now that Donnie had let Trey go with Brian on the Disney World trip that Kimberly's church was sponsoring, Max felt he was compelled to join this particular special, late Saturday night gathering.

They all started the evening dancing and drinking and looking at the hoochies at Donnie's Lounge that was adjacent to his gym. At about midnight, the players who were now gathered around the table had all drifted upstairs through an exit door that led to Donnie's private quarters. Donnie brought Max up.

"Hey, man ... neat place!" he said, stepping through the door into a large kitchen in what looked like it had once been a warehouse, with brick walls and stainless steel. To the right of the room was the dimly-lit cooking area, separated from the larger, brighter dining area by a bar with six stools. A custom-made, long, red, leather couch was on the opposite wall. In the center of it was a built-in chest shaped like a pyramid, so that the couch looked like back to back chaise lounges. A couple of guys sat on the divan sharing a joint when Max and Donnie entered. Two others were seated at the table, drinking beers and playing a two-hand round.

"Yeah. It suits me well," Donnie said. "Hey... let's step in here for a minute, while I get a little something special for the head." He led Max down a dimly-lit hall lined with sensual modern art on both walls to the last room on the left, and opened the door.

Max stepped in.

"Be right back," Donnie closed the door.

Max turned and looked about the dimly-lit room. In it, Max could see a full bed and a tilted mirror hanging by a golden tassel over a writing desk. There was an armoire, and a couple of chairs at a table by the window where floor-length, leather, ribbon curtains hung. It was an understated, yet well appointed, thoroughly masculine room. Standing at the window, Max admired the feel of the smooth leather pieces as he peered out.

"You like the leather ribbons?" Donnie asked coming back into the room.

"Yeah, man." Max turned, letting the leather ribbon curtains fall, coming to Donnie. "I've never seen any thing like that, before," he added.

"That's because I designed them," Donnie said, handing Max a joint, and firing up his own. He took a toke and held it while holding the lighter for Max. "And a whole lot of other pieces you'll see around here. I must have been a damn decorator, or furniture designer, or something in another life," he laughed.

So did Max. And in a matter of minutes he was feeling mellow.

And Donnie could tell

"Ready to join the game?!" he asked.

"Yeah man," Max replied, laughingly.

"Well, com'on! Let me take some of that *boot-tae* you got in those pants... pockets!" Donnie said, jovially, opening the door.

"Meet Joe Goode," the bigger of the two guys Max had seen at the table when they first came in, nodded. "And Slim Reed."

"Hey, man."

"Pleased to meet you," Max said, taking Slim Reed's hand.

"I hope your ass still feel that way after I take all yo' dough!" Slim said, and sat back down.

They all laughed.

They played poker.

A little later that night, with a couple of winning pots in his pocket and a jovial mood all around, Max was feeling at ease when Donnie returned to the table with a third round of drinks. He set Max's drink down, last. Max didn't notice when Donnie, smoothly, moved into the shadows behind where he sat, watching the game, and Max.

By his third winning hand, Max was feeling great. He thought it was because of his winning streak. He finished the drink Donnie had placed before him. Taking the cards to deal, this time he fumbled the shuffle.

"Mannn, yo-yo'ass is drunk! Give me the fucking cards!" the player next to him said, laughing, taking the cards from Max.

Max stood, dropping some money. Donnie picked it up.

"Where's the bathroom?" Max asked. "I've gotta... I've gotta...."

"I'll show you," Donnie said, taking his prey's arm, momentarily, to steady him.

Max followed Donnie back down the darkened hallway.

Max stumbled into the large, ornate, black and gold bathroom. He managed to get his pants down and urinated before he realized that the noise he heard wasn't still coming from the guys in the kitchen, but from the flat-screen television on the wall! It was on, and it was showing him being taken by one of his masters when he was at the Lodge!

Suddenly he felt like he was dreaming as he stood there, wobbly—trying to clear his head. By the time he realized he wasn't dreaming, he realized Donnie was standing close behind him.

"Let me help you with that," he whispered into Max's ear.

Taking Max's rapidly-growing cock in one hand, Donnie slipped a hard, rubber cock-ring onto it, pulled his cock through it, roughly, and quickly rolled it along the shaft until it fitted snuggly against Max's bulging balls!

Drugged and drunk, Max struggled to fight him off, as Donnie forced Max's pants down around his ankles. But even as he struggled, with Donnie's touch he felt that sudden white-hot desire stir so deep within his loins he couldn't contain the moan that escaped from somewhere equally as deep within him!

Still, his mind told him to pull away from what it felt he wouldn't be able to resist. He tried. But, instead of getting away from Donnie, he stumbled falling to the floor face down.

Then, Donnie was on him.

And as it was happening, Max couldn't believe he was being raped, again!

But, he was.

"I'm getting this ass, tonight, baby!" Donnie said, easily forcing Max's sneakers and pants off. "I know what it can take! I've tasted it, before! I know how sweet this is! And … I've been wanting more ever since!" he whispered, holding Max down with one hand, and inserting a plastic syringe filled with lube into his prey's waiting anus with the other.

Max inhaled, deeply. His head was spinning from the drugs and the liquor, and from realizing what was happening to him. He was hearing this, and he wasn't. All he could feel was his entire being being consumed by the overwhelming desire he could no longer control. A low sigh escaped his lips again as the syringe entered.

"Aahhhh! …. Wha-what-are-ya-doin to me, man?!" he managed to ask, in a voice a little too meek for his own taste.

He knew.

"Making you my bitch, mutha-fucka! I told you I'm getting this boot-tae tonight! I'm getting ready to fuck your brains out, tonight, baby!" Donnie exclaimed, slapping Max's tense buns, hard, while slathering oil on them, and onto his own huge, 6" diameter, 13" long cock.

Now, he moved between Max's legs. "I know what this ass-pussy can take, baby.... 'Cause I keep going over every minute I had it at the Lodge! Every fuckin' minute!" he said, placing the head of his huge, rock-hard cock to Max's squirming ass. And, with one powerful thrust the head of his huge mass disappeared inside.

"Whooaaahhhh!" Max cried out! "Uuhhh.... Uuhhh! Uh.............." he moaned with each thrust.

He moaned and cried out again and again and again, as Donnie slowly, methodically, drove his huge member deeper and deeper into his giving tunnel.

Max's head was swirling. He was being consumed by the erotic pain entering him. Yet, he was feeling the satisfaction of having that thirst deep within once again being fulfilled. He didn't want Donnie to stop, even if his mind told him he did. Torn, he couldn't help himself. And, hearing his moans from the television, and feeling the big cock consuming him, he couldn't control the moans and cries escaping from his lips now. He felt erotically, helplessly out of control.

"Oohhh... noooo..." he moaned. He was totally in his own head when the knowledge of the hidden desire he had desperately tried to escape from, once again consumed him completely, forcing him to once again give himself over to the pure, wanton acceptance of this desire that refused to stay hidden.

"Oh, yes!" Donnie whispered, erotically, rhythmically pumping Max, each time ramming his cock deeper into him! "Yeessss!"

Donnie moaned too, between plunging, ramming and caressing the tight, deep brown ass before him. He wanted to watch his cock sink into his prey's tightness, but every time the head of it reached a ring of muscle, it slowed his penetration to a halt, forcing him to bend over onto Max's back to maintain control. Like he had said, he knew Max could take every inch he had to give. And he knew he would give it all tonight!

"Aahhh... baby! Don't fight it! It's sooo tight! Sooo hot... sooo thick, baby! So deep and gooood!" he licked into Max's ear, sending his tongue in and around, and biting his earlobe. "It's good! And I've been wanting this ass for a long time, baby!" Then, almost as suddenly, "I'm gonna fuck the shit out of your

51

tight ass, tonight, bitch! I'm gonna fuck the shit out of you!" he hissed. He was back up, now, plunging his cock in deeper.

"Whooaaahhhhh!" Max cried out, breathlessly. "Pleaseee.... Noooo!" he moaned.

"No!" Donnie exclaimed. "I know you! And I know what you want, baby! What you can take!"

"Oohhh-aahhhh! Nooo...." Max managed to make himself utter, again.

"Oohhh-yeessss! I know this ass... and I'm gonna make you my bitch tonight, baby ... 'cause I know what it can take.... Uuhhhh... uuhhhh!" Donnie moaned, "and... I'm gonna make you my ass-pussy bitch, baby!"

"Aahhhh...." Max cried. He knew he had felt the erotic pain of this huge dick filling him, before. He knew Donnie S. Williams had to have been the Number 1 who had fucked him at the Lodge that last night!

"I know how much you like having a big, hard dick in your ass, baby.... I could feel it!"

"Nooo...." Max cried.

"You can say that shit!" Donnie hissed as a sudden anger consumed him. "But ... I know you.... I know this some good ass, baby! And I know you want this big, hard dick in your ass, don't you?!" He plunged it deeper into him.

"Oohhh-aahhhh! God... aahhhh!"

"Don't you?!" Donnie demanded with another hard plunge. His huge cock was half-way into Max's anus now. "Don't you, bitch?!" he asked, again slapping Max's bun so hard it stung his hand and instantly left a reddish imprint on the deep brown bun where it landed.

"Ooohhh... God! Yessss!" Max moaned, and cried, humiliated at being made to admit it aloud.

Again, Donnie slapped his butt and rammed his cock into his hot, tight, trembling ass.

"Aahhhh, baby, this ass's sooo good!" he moaned. On the verge of cumming, Donnie could no longer contain himself. "I knew this ass was this good, baby! I... I... aahhhhhh! You got a sweet ass, baby! A sweet, mutha-fucking ass!" he moaned when he could no longer control it.

The cum shot fast and hot from him with such force, it pushed him back!

He reached around and underneath his prostrated, moaning prey, and gripping Max's cock at the base, he forced his ass back up against him to keep from being dislodged.

"Damn, baby! Damn!" he said, as he rolled Max over onto his side so that both were lying on their sides.

Still cumming, Donnie rolled Max's cock-ring off. And, pumping Max's cock like he was pumping his own, Max's cum shot from him like white-hot bullets!

"Aahhhh, yes... aahhhh, yes... aahhhh, yes," he sighed, with each explosion.

And, with that, Max's head stopped swirling, and his world went black.

But, for Donnie, everything was just beginning.

"Hey!" he yelled, "you get everything?" he asked the cameraman, who had videotaped the entire encounter.

"Got it all right here," he replied, patting the digital camcorder.

Now, the other peeping *card players* entered.

"That looked good, man."

"Damn! You fucked that ass! You tore it up, mane!"

"Shit, man! That was real deep!" the third one said, all complimenting Donnie.

Yeah. But, not deep enough. Not all the way, Donnie thought. He had gotten up, and was tying the belt on his short, black, silk robe. Max was out, still lying on the floor where he left him.

"Put him in the room," he ordered and motioned toward the bedrooms. "And clean his ass up. It ain't over!" he said. "He's getting all this tonight," he was motioning to his cock. It hung huge, even in a relaxed mode. "Make sure everything's everything... and get the hair off his ass!" he added, "I want to see what I'm fucking.... And boys, make sure you keep him feeling good," he ordered.

And with that, Donnie showered, dressed and went back down to his lounge, along with several of the card players.

But there were four who hung back to follow Donnie's orders. One of them was the cameraman. Grabbing him underneath each arm, two lifted Max's limp, naked body and took him into the bedroom. The camera was steadily on his anus, the oil and Donnie's cum seeping out of it made it shine. In the room, one of them spread a clean towel on the California-king bed, and they laid him face up on it.

One came in with what appeared to be a portable hospital basin filled with soapy water, sudded him up and then shaved him. While another placed a tray, with several large jars of lubricants, oils and plastic syringes on it, on a table at the foot of the bed. The third placed a large, clear, smooth Lucite, slant-board in the center of the large bed. The sides and the high end were open and placing himself on his back, he slid his head underneath it, just so. Then, the other two managed to lay totally inebriated and semi-conscious, naked Max over onto the slant-board so that his cock and balls hung down to a hot, waiting mouth, below, as the camera focused close up on it entering it.

The one who washed him was now naked. He lay to one side of Max. And using his unusually long tongue, he began licking and sucking Max's balls.

The one who had brought in the tray was also naked now. He was on his knees on the other side, and using his hands to hold Max's firm buns open, he used his tongue to rim his pulsating anus, licking and sucking it like the was eating an ice-cream cone.

Unable to control any aspect of this deliriously ecstatic situation, Max felt like he was having a wet dream, and his body was reacting to every sensation—both individually, and all at once.

Were it not for Max's soul-satisfying moans and cries filling the room they might have heard the beat from the dance floor below, where Donnie was dancing sensuously triumphant, with Sharon.

* * * *

But only Donnie could hear her whisper in his ear:

"Oohhh, I can see, you're loving that ass, baby…. And believe me, he's loving it too! So, you can tell me it's the best ass you've ever had. Don't I always get the best for you?! You know, I want you to have the best... because... I love you, baby. I'll always love you."

* * * *

The cameraman was replacing the disk when Donnie reappeared, again wearing only his short robe. His hardening cock fell further down his thighs. They were still pleasuring Max who had been slipping in and out of a drug-induced, erotically semi-consciousness. He didn't know that Donnie had returned. That is, until that huge cock once again pierced every fiber of his being with such depth and force that it left his body rigid and shaking involuntarily for as long as Donnie applied pressure. And he applied it for almost a full minute before he eased up and allowed both Max, and himself, to breathe. Now he began to slowly guide his huge, heavy member deeper into Max.

"You knew I'd be back, didn't you, baby?" he asked. "I told you, you're getting all this tonight... every inch of it! And... if I have to... I'm gonna beat this ass until you take it all in!" he swore. He gave each of Max's helpless buns several stinging slaps, and then thrust his big cock deep into him! He continued slapping Max's ass as he drove it deeper into Max's quivering, giving tunnel.

A painful moan escaped from Max after each blow. His body was involuntarily tensing and relaxing after each one, allowing Donnie's cock to go deeper with each stroke.

"Aahhhh... this some good ass-pussy!" Donnie cried through deep breaths, "I'm gonna make this my ass-pussy, tonight! Can I make this my ass-pussy, baby?! Can I make you my bitch?! Can I make this my ass-pussy?!" Donnie settled into an insistent murmuring and an intense thrusting.

And, Max was breathing hard too, crying out at each slap and thrust! But helplessly accepting it all.

"Can I make this my ass-pussy, baby?!" Donnie asked, again landing a hard slap to first Max's right bun, and another to his left! "Can I make you my ass-pussy, bitch?!.... Answer me! Dammit!" Another stinging slap and another powerful plunge! "Can I make this my ass-pussy?!"

"Aahhh! Nooo... pleaseee!..... Pleaseee!! I—I hate this shit, man!" Max cried.

Donnie slapped his ass even harder. "Can I make this my ass-pussy, bitch?!" he demanded. "Can I, nigga?!" He sent his huge, hard cock as deep as it could go into Max, and held it there.

"Goddd!!! Nooo! Aahhh... nooo, man!....." Then, "Yesss!.... Yeahhh... man!" Max managed to cry. "Yessss.... Goddd... mannn!"

Donnie heard what he wanted to he hear.

"Call me Big Daddy when I'm fucking you in your ass!" Donnie demanded, landing more open-handed slaps to Max's ass and thrusting his huge rod deeper into him. "You're going to feel these balls in your ass again, tonight, baby! You want me put these balls in your ass, tonight?!"

The others had moved away when Donnie first mounted Max, but they hadn't left the bed. Now, they were watching Donnie and Max, erotically excited, as they sucked and fucked each other. But, the cameraman was still shooting Donnie and Max's asses up close. Now, Donnie used his powerful legs and thighs to part Max's thighs even wider.

"Suck his dick! Give'em some head!" he ordered, and one of them quickly went between their legs underneath the slant-board and took Max's hard, throbbing cock into his mouth.

"Sssss... aaahhhh!" Max murmured.

Donnie, resting on his knees, had 8 inches inside Max. He landed several more, painfully hard blows to each trembling, accepting bun, simultaneously, each strike eliciting breathless cries from both of them.

"Call me Big Daddy when I'm fucking your ass, bitch! Now—call me Big Daddy!"

"Big—Big Daddy!" Max cried.

"Can I make this my ass-pussy?! Now... call me Big Daddy!" he groaned, driving his massive cock deeper into Max's hot, tight, gaping anus.

"Yesssss, Big Daddy," Max cried, sweat pouring off him. "Yesssss, Big Daddy!"

"Damn right!" Donnie hissed, while ramming his rock-hard member in again and again. "Damn right... this my hot.. tight ass, ass-pussy! And... you gonna let me fuck it?! You gonna give it to me, baby?! You gonna give it to your Big Daddy whenever I want it!"

"Yesssss, Big Daddy! Yessss!" Max exclaimed, unable to stop his tight hole from being forced open by the huge, demanding force within it. Exonerating himself in the excruciatingly erotic pain of it all was knowing he had no control over any of it—he was entering a zone. The same zone he had only viewed on video and couldn't stop revisiting in his mind ever since leaving the Lodge.

"Don't stop! Keep saying it!" Donnie demanded, sending another couple of blows onto Max's right bun. "Call me Big Daddy!" he shouted, he was riding Max like he was riding a horse. All of his cock was buried inside Max, now.

"Yesssss, Big Daddy... yesssss, Big Daddy... yessss, Big Daddy...." Max continued to cry with every suck, every lick, every caress and every painful thrust.

Soon, if you were looking in the camera you would have seen Donnie's balls tightened as he sank and held every inch of himself all the way in Max. Slowly sinking in and pulling out and feeling every throbbing, ecstasy-filled vibration of his captive's body, he knew he would soon blow.

"Get the ring off! Get the ring off and suck him! Drink him down! He's cumming! Aahhhh... I'm cumming! Oohhh baby!" Donnie cried. "I'm gonna blow... I'm gonna cum! I'm gonna cum.... Can I cum in your ass?! Aahhhh! Aahhhh! I'm cumming, baby!" he sighed. "You've got all of this! Aahhhh! Your ass's sooo good, baby! It's good!"

Max felt his insides grow even hotter and quivery, as Donnie exploded, pumping his juices deep inside him. Max could not tell whether the cries he was hearing were coming from himself or from Donnie. What he was experiencing he unwittingly knew was the feeling he craved and loved, even if it was the feeling he wanted to hate. But, where his mind could waver, his body couldn't deny it. And when the cock-ring was snapped, he felt the hot, quivering quake of receiving an orgasm deeper than anything he had ever felt within him, while his muscle pumped his own cum deep down the hot, receiving throat beneath him!

"Yessss!.... Aahhh, yes! Big Daddy...." he moaned.

Chapter VI

The next morning Max was awake before he felt he could open his eyes. He was lying on his back, and though he had several starts at turning and lifting his body, he felt he couldn't do it. For a minute he felt as though a weight had been placed on him. So, he lay back with his eyes closed, focusing on what had happened the night before. He knew Donnie had drugged and raped him. And though his stuff still ached, for him that morning, it was a nauseatingly sweet ache. His mind still couldn't wrap itself around that, though.

He brought his left hand up across his body, and massaged the back of his neck. He opened his eyes. Then slowly he sat up. He was naked, and he was alone in the room. And, with sunlight streaming through the cracks in the ribbon curtains, once again, an ambivalent guilt consumed him.

What are you doing, man? Why?! Why do you keep letting this shit happen? You know you're letting it happen, don't you? You knew before you came it was going to happen, didn't you?! Why? You? You! Why do you want it? You fag?

No, I'm not! retorted the other voice in his head.

Then, get dressed, and get the fuck out of here! And, never come back, man! The voices dueled.

* * * *

Donnie was wearing sweatpants, a tank, and a headband with a towel around his neck. He was seated at an amply set table having breakfast alone when Max, trying to find his way out unnoticed, found himself in the kitchen. He was fully dressed now, in the clothes he had worn the night before. He had found them neatly folded on the table where the tray had been placed sometime the night before.

Donnie didn't get up. And, to Max's surprise, he heard Donnie's voice before he saw him.

"Come have some breakfast, man… you got some money over here," he said, expectantly, while looking at Max and wiping his mouth with a corner of the towel.

Trying not to show his disappointment at being caught, Max was at least glad Donnie had spoken first. He didn't know what he would have said, had he not. He tensed, not knowing what to say—or do.

He had totally forgotten about the game, much less the money he had won. He had been trying to escape and he felt scared, but he was determined not to let Donnie see it. He was hungry—and he wanted the money—and, he wanted to prove to himself and to Donnie that he wasn't scared. He came to the table, put some sausage, grits and eggs on a plate, sat down and started eating, without saying a word.

"Five hundred," Donnie placed the money on the table beside him.

It was more than Max remembered winning. But he didn't remember much about the card game. He took the money, folded it and stuffed it in his pocket.

He still didn't say anything. He couldn't look at Donnie.

"I've got something else here," Donnie continued, placing a disk on the table. "You were good, last night, my man…. Damn fuckin' good! So good, in fact, they're burning these, right now…." He held up the disk. "Here's your copy," he said, and slide the disk toward Max.

Max wasn't surprised about a video being made. He was surprised that Donnie Williams would ever let anyone see him doing a man. But, he concealed his surprise, and kept on eating.

"We're selling the edited one," Donnie continued as if reading his mind. "It's darker, and they could scramble the faces a bit."

Now, Max looked at him.

"But this one was cut from the original. You can see everything," he continued, steadily, driving his point home.

And Max knew exactly what he meant. He started eating again.

"Now, I'm going to tell you how we're going to do this thing," Donnie's voice was dead serious. He was buttering another piece of bread, arrogantly nonchalant. "You're gonna come work for me."

He popped a piece of bread into his mouth, chewed and swallowed it before he continued, looking at Max the whole while. "You see, I want you in my life, baby… because… my dick loves your hot stuff! I gotta have it in my life…." He was leaning towards Max, rubbing his knee, now.

Max moved his knee away from Donnie's hand.

And Donnie straightened up. "You start Monday morning—after you take your boy to school," he said, wiping his hands with the towel.

Max was stunned! He was trying to hide his feelings, and he didn't know whether it was from Donnie's hand or his words. He couldn't eat anymore. He said nothing. He didn't know what to say. He felt an erotic queasiness in his stomach.

"I'll pay you a grand a week. You'll be my... let's say, personal assistant.. attendant...." Donnie kind of chuckled as he said this. "Attending to me, only," he said, and took another bite while looking at Max. "You'll be here whenever I need you to be here."

"Wh—what if I don't want the job, man?" Max's question sounded more like a plea. He still couldn't bring himself to look at Donnie.

Donnie chuckled.

"It's not like you have much of a choice," he said. "You see, I get what I want... always! And besides... you already got the j-o-b!" his voice was low and menacing as he spelled the word.

Now he got up and stood behind Max, who was still seated at the table. His hands were on Max's shoulders.

"I do this because I want this sweet, hot ass, baby! I've wanted it again, ever since I got it the first time up at the Lodge.... Man! I mean... first time my dick was hitting everything just right! I want the ass, baby, 'cause I like the way my dick feels when it's slammin' it...." He smiled, massaging Max's shoulders. "And you like it too. The body don't lie, baby. The body can't hide what it likes... what it wants... needs!"

"I pick my son up after school, man!" Max said, cutting him off, without looking up from his plate. And, immediately he wished he hadn't said anything.

"Yeah. And you will pick my son up, too, mutha-fucka. Then, you will take them both to practice. Then, you'll take them home. You know, things a personal assistant would do. And then you'll come back here until *our* work is done. Most nights you should be able to get home by 11:00... midnight at the latest," adding, "... if you want to go," he whispered.

Donnie had heard the helplessness in Max's voice, and he knew that Max knew he couldn't refuse his offer.

60

"You want to see your son in the majors, don't you? I can get him there.... But, you've gotta play ball with me, baby.... You're gonna play ball with me."

He bent over so his mouth was close to Max's ear and his hands were down to Max's crouch. Massaging and squeezing, he continued, "It's like you're my... catcher, baby.... I think your sweet ass can catch everything I pitch at it! Don't you?"

Feeling Donnie's breathe behind him, his hands expertly and painfully working between his legs, Max closed his eyes trying to steel himself to the feeling, and said nothing.

"Now, don't make me have to kick your ass again, nigga!" Donnie whispered in his ear, and from his closeness alone, Max knew he meant it.

There was no doubt in Max's mind that Donnie could take him. Max thought he was at least 5 years younger. He was a few inches taller, and his athletic, chiseled physique left no question in Max's mind as to what that outcome would be.

"What if I don't want this shit, man?" Max whispered, sincerely. "I mean, I'm— I'm no fa...."

"Neither am I!" Donnie hissed, cutting him off. "I'm not saying you're a punk. I'm saying I don't consummate a deal unless I know exactly what I'm getting, baby. Besides, I've told you what you are!" he said. "You're my.. personal assistant."

He was stroking and squeezing Max's hardening cock, passionately, now.

"You want this," he growled. "But I see, you just want to be one of those fuckin', conventional mutha-fuckas.... You feel guilty wanting it in the ass. So, you got to have it like this!...."

Bending over from behind him, with both hands he suddenly grabbed Max's balls and twisted them, tight, each in the opposite direction and holding them that way!

"Ooaaaahhhhhh!!" Max groaned. The pain was so sudden and intense, Max saw stars! He couldn't move! His body could only surrender to the pain. He couldn't believe the intensity! "Pleasseeee, man! Aahhhhh..." he cried out in agony!

"Call me Big Daddy!" Donnie hissed, squeezing them once more.

"Big Daddy! Big Daddy!" Max's cry came fast.

And, Donnie let go.

"Is that the way you want it, baby?" Donnie licked into his ear, then did it again just as suddenly, just as painfully.

"Nooo! Pleaseeee Man!" Max's pled, and again his body went to the paralyzing pain once more.

"You want it!—But, you got to have it pleading…" Donnie twisted Max's balls even tighter!

And with that, like an explosion, he grabbed Max's arm and snatched him from the chair! In the process, turning the chair over and sending Max to the smooth, cool, stone kitchen floor!

Donnie was on him, again.

With his left hand, Donnie forced Max's left arm back, and held it there pinning him face down.

Dazed and breathless, Max hadn't seen it coming. He didn't have time to resist.

Donnie was on top of him, tugging at his own pants and pulling them down far enough to take out his huge, hardening cock. Then, he pulled Max's pants down below his knees.

Straddling him, Donnie stuck his huge, engorged, chocolate phallus between Max's thighs. Pending Max's left arm to his back, Donnie landed a painfully hard slap to Max's tight buttocks.

"Ooaaaahhhhh… noooooaaaahhhhhh!" Max cried, but he didn't resist.

Hearing the truth of Donnie's words, and knowing what was again about to happen, there wasn't much fight left in him.

"Ooaaaahhhhh… yeesssss!" Donnie said, mockingly, and quickly sent another powerful blow to his right bun! "Want me to make it hurt more than this, bitch?! I can make it hurt more than this!"

"Pleasseeee… nooooooaaaahhhhhh…" Max moaned, his body squirming, tensing and giving in, as sweat burst forth from all over his body; and tears, of what he felt as the humiliatingly painful sensuousness of it, teamed in his eyes.

Max wanted to hate Donnie for making him do what he told himself he didn't want to do. He felt humiliated with himself for cumming every time Donnie took him. Yet, he found himself unable to resist the desire Donnie stirred in him.

Somewhere deep within his gut, Max knew he had to have the pain. He wanted Donnie to hurt him because the pain absolved him of the guilt he felt for his craving—his desire. So, Donnie beat him. And Max couldn't stop himself from finding the pain and the sex exquisitely deliciously fulfilling.

And, Donnie was enjoying beating him.

Max's ass burned like it was on fire. The floor beneath him was wet from his tears, sweat and soon his and Donnie's juices.

"Ooaaaahhhhhh... pleasseeee, Big Daddy!" he cried, squirming, tensing and giving in beneath each squeeze, twist or blow.

"You'll... be... here... by... 8:30... Monday... morning.... Won't... you... you...ass... pussy... bitch!" Donnie hissed, landing a blow between almost every word.

"Ooaaahhhhhh.... Noooo..... Man...." Max moaned.

"Call... me... Big... Daddy!" Donnie demanded and slapped Max's ass, again, "...when I'm fuckin' yo'ass!"

"Ooaaaahhhhhh... Big Daddy!" Max moaned, openly sobbing.

"Call me Big Daddy, dammit!" Donnie continued.

"Yeessss—Yeessss... Big Daddy!"

"Keep saying it! Dammit! Keep on calling me Big Daddy!" Donnie demanded.

"Yeesss... Big Daddy.... Yesss... Big Daddy...." Max cried.

Stretching, Donnie was reaching for the butter dish on top of the table. He placed it on the floor beside them, scooped up a handful, and slathered it onto his own hand and fore-arm, and, into Max's anus.

And the next thing Max felt was the searing delirium of penetration!

Donnie easily slid his hand and his wrist in first, pumping Max that way! His own delirium coming from feeling complete possession of the hot, wet quivering inside of his yielding prey!

"Uuhuh!.... Oohhhh... Godddd!" Max cried.

But, that morning Donnie didn't stop until his balls were slamming against Max's ass over-and-over, again, once more!

63

"This is *your* last tango in Paris, baby! You'll never be the same after this fuck!"

And with that, Donnie banged Max for another hard, hot, sweaty 5 minutes before he exploded in Max's wet, burning-hot ass.

Donnie gave his cheeks a few more smacks when he got off him. Then he casually picked up the towel that had fallen from round his neck, as he straightened up and stretched holding the towel in both hands high above his head.

"Do me wrong and the whole world will know where you live and… what you are, you sweet-ass bitch!" he said, standing over Max. He dropped the towel on Max's back. "Now, dry your ass off, and take yo'ass home. Just be here on Monday morning."

Naked, Donnie left the kitchen, leaving Max lying there in an aching heap.

No one came to his rescue, but he correctly suspected that the morning's whole scenario was probably being videotaped. Aching, trying to pull himself together, he felt ashamed—yet, totally satiated.

Slowly, quietly, he did as he was told—dressed and left.

Later that day at home, Max eased himself into his Epsom salt bath. His whole body was sore, and he hoped he wouldn't bruise. He didn't know how he would explain that to Kimberly. He immersed himself in the water, then, laid his head back to think.

He felt trapped. He knew he had no choice but to give in to Donnie's demand, or suffer the consequences of being outed to the world, to Kimberly and, to his son for having willingly taken part in a lifestyle he thought he had walked away from. But as he lay there, soaking wet, he knew he had been brought back into that life. And he knew that come early Monday morning he would report to Donnie, as ordered.

Chapter VII

"The man's having breakfast, upstairs," a guy polishing glasses working behind the bar said to Max as he entered Donnie's darkened bar that bright Monday morning. "He said to tell you to come on up," he added.

Slowly, Max went up the stairs and through the exit door that was the entrance to Donnie's private chambers. He found Donnie seated at the kitchen table having breakfast like before. Today, he was shirtless again with a towel around his neck.

Seated next to him, also eating breakfast, was one of the prettiest men Max had ever laid eyes on.

"Come in, Max," Donnie called when Max came through the door. "Meet Pretty Boy."

Max and Pretty Boy glanced at each other; neither spoke. In that glance, Max could instantly tell that Pretty Boy was indeed as queer as he was beautiful.

"Have a seat. Have some breakfast," Donnie said, as Max came to the table on the other side of him, opposite Pretty Boy.

"I've had breakfast," he replied, taking a seat.

"Good!" Donnie said, wiping his hands on the towel without taking his eyes off Max. "We're about finished, anyway. Pretty Boy here is going to take you to your room… office. He'll show you the ropes. Doc Stewart's gonna be here at 10. I've got to test you, baby… gotta keep it clean."

Max thought about the last time he had been seen by a doctor. He knew this time would be no different. He sat motionless, listening to Donnie, but not looking at him.

"In the meantime, get to know the Lodge," Donnie continued, "Pretty Boy will make you comfortable, keep you feeling good. Won't you?" Donnie asked, now looking at Pretty Boy.

Pretty Boy took a napkin and dabbed each corner of his mouth, looking at Max with a knowing smile on his face.

"I'll be in to see how you're doing a little later," Donnie finished.

And with that, Pretty Boy pushed his chair back and got up from the table.

"Com'on, baby," he said to Max in a voice more feminine even than his looks. He stood and came around the table behind Donnie, to Max. "The master has spoken." He switched off and Max got up and following him.

* * * *

"Turn that off!" Max ordered Pretty Boy later that morning when they came into the room where he and Donnie had smoked, to find the television in the armoire blasting a video of Donnie doing him at the Lodge.

"Uh-un!" Pretty Boy whined. "We've been looking at him pounding your ass every since he first got a taste of it at the Lodge! Shit, it's like background music now, baby."

Pretty Boy stood at the chest of drawers with his back to Max. There was a mini-bar on top of it, and he was pouring drinks, mixing a little white powder into the one he was making for Max. He continued talking with his back to him.

"I think he's been after your stuff every since the Lodge," he said, finishing the drinks, he turned and brought it to Max. "You've got a lot to learn, baby," he said, handing it to him.

He took the drink and sat on the edge of the bed, looking at the television.

Pretty Boy sipped his drink and stared at the action on the television, too. It was showing Donnie banging Max on the kitchen floor.

"You may as well get used to drinking... or doing whatever it takes for you," Pretty Boy said, turning his own drink up while looking at the TV. "'Cause he really loves putting that big, fuckin' dick of his in that ass, baby," he said, cutting his eyes at Max. "And, he'll soon be here for so' more."

Hearing that, Max turned the drink up.

"Uummm... I see he gave you the biggest room... I mean office," Pretty Boy continued, coyly looking at him, then walking around the room. "You've got your own, private bathroom in here," he opened the door to the bathroom. "A beautiful view..." he pulled the leather, ribbon curtains back to show the front view from the building. "Though, I doubt you'll get a chance to see much of that. Your closet," he opened the closet door and thumbed through its content. "A couple of robes... a couple of *Donnie's Place* sweats.... But I guess that's

66

just about all the wardrobe you'll be needing for this job," he said in his sing-song voice, subtly looking for and   seeing the affect the drink was having on Max. "Now," he continued, coming back over to the chest of drawers, "let's see if he still keeps his dong stash down here."   He opened the bottom drawer. "Oohhh, yeah!" he exclaimed, pulling out a huge, black, rubber dildo. "Donnie's dick was the model for this one!" he exclaimed, holding it up in front of Max with both hands.

The 13" dildo looked humongous to Max.   In fact, it looked like two.   He was seeing double by now, that dizzy feeling he had come to know.   He was trying to contain himself, determined not to let Pretty Boy see his surprise at seeing such a huge cock—even if it was a dildo.

But Pretty Boy could see the affect his drink—and the dildo—were having on Max.

"This one is Donnie," he said, lovingly running his tongue along the shaft of it, before easing it back into the drawer.

"Why don't you get comfortable, baby?   Donnie wants me to make sure you're comfortable," he said, coming to Max now.

He bent down and removed Max's shoes.   Sensually, he let his hands caress Max's legs as he lifted them onto the bed.   And Max let him bring his hands to his waist and loosen his belt.   Max let Pretty Boy unbutton his pants and pull them down, revealing the uncontrollable hardness of his anticipation.

"What… was in the drink?" Max asked as Pretty Boy took off his own shirt and tossed it aside.

Next, on his knees, Pretty Boy was forcing Max's hard cock through a rubber cock-ring.

"Something Donnie got especially for you, baby," Pretty Boy murmured as he engulfed the entire length of Max's shaft!

"Aahhhhhh… whooahhhh!" Max sighed as Pretty Boy held him in the back of his throat, gargling and swallowing over and over again, teasing the head of the engorged cock.

"Aahhhhhh! Damn! Whooahhhh!" came Max's erotic moans while Pretty Boy worked on him and the drink sent him into another dimension. He placed a hand on Pretty Boy's head and closed his eyes.

His own head was swirling!

He couldn't think of anything right now, except what was happening to him. So engrossed in receiving Pretty Boy's oral pleasures, he didn't realize Donnie had joined them until he heard him speak.

"You like that hot throat, baby?!" Donnie whispered in his ear.

"Yes... yeesss!" Max moaned, breathlessly.

"You see how good I can make you feel, huh?"

"Yeesss," Max groaned. His eyes were closed. He felt Donnie's hands on his shoulders, pushing him down onto the bed.

"Call me Big Daddy when I'm letting a nigga suck your dick," he ordered, moving so that he was close to Max's mouth. He lightly slapped his cheek to emphasize his point.

Max blinked, opened his eyes. He looked dead into Donnie's. And Donnie could see the erotic surrender in his eyes, as Pretty Boy continued working on him. It was what he wanted to see.

He smiled. "Call me Big Daddy," he ordered, again.

"Yeesss, Big Daddy," Max obeyed.

Then, Donnie sent his tongue down Max's throat. And Max took his kisses.

Slowly, Donnie's kisses moved to Max's throat. Then, to his nipples where his teeth pulled at the hardened, brown bumps, until they felt and looked like red-hot coals. Then, he moved down to his naval swirling the tip of his tongue around and around until it hit center, and darted in and out several times before ending in a powerful suck that made Max's entire body quiver.

Max moaned, loudly.

Lifting Max's leg, Donnie went around Pretty Boy to get to Max's balls, licking, nibbling and sucking them, and using his fingers to rim him.

"Leave us," he ordered, finally, when he was sure Pretty Boy's concoction was taking full affect on Max.

Max lay moaning. He found himself in a strange consciousness, his body helplessly enjoying every erotic sensation, his mind not wanting, yet, wanting, and completely unable to resist.

With his mouth, Pretty Boy gave Max's cock a few more purposely painfully powerful pulls before he let go. Leaving the bed, he grabbed his shirt and sashayed toward the door.

"Make sure they're getting this," Donnie said, before Pretty Boy closed it.

Still working Max's balls with his tongue, Donnie took lubricant from a jar, Max would soon learn he had them strategically placed about the Lodge, and slathered it onto his mammoth member. Next, he packed a handful of lube into Max's anus. He moved so that he was sitting on the side of the bed with his feet on the floor. Cupping his arms underneath Max's thighs and leaning back, Donnie pulled him around onto his lap. Holding his legs wide open, Donnie impelled Max forcing him down onto the head of his rock-hard rod!

Oohhhaahhhhh!" Max cried, arching his head back. Max was not a small guy, and it amazed him at how easily Donnie was handling him.

"You can take it, baby!" Donnie ordered, reaching around in front of him, grabbing his balls with both hands. He twisted them in the agonizing way Max had come to know all too well.

"Pleaseeee! Big Daddy.... Pleaseeee!" he cried, losing his own strength as his body tensed and gripped the huge rod he was fast sinking onto.

"Aahhhh... yessss!" Donnie moaned. He let go, then twisted Max's balls, again. "You want me to hurt you, don't you, baby?! You want me to take it from you... like this!"

Max violently threw back his head. "Goddd! Pleaseeee... Big Daddy!..." he moaned, helplessly, as every inch of Donnie's huge cock disappeared inside him.

"Mmmm... this ass is sooo good, baby! Your ass is sooo mutha-fuckin' good!" Donnie licked into Max's ear, as he twisted and released his balls again and again. Forcing Max's body to tense, gripping and releasing his throbbing shaft again and again and again. Until, trembling, he wrapped his arms around Max's waist, holding him fast down onto his rod and using the muscles in his legs, Donnie pumped Max for as long as he could!

"Hold it, baby! Whoooaaa! Don't move.... Shit! Stop!" Donnie breathed the words out through his teeth.

And Max felt Donnie's fire-hot cum shooting into him. Cum so hot, he felt it's heat spreading, filling his entire being.

"Uummm... aahhh, baby!" Donnie moaned, "that's soooo fuckin' good! Uh-uh-uh! Got all this dick! Your ass is sooo fuck-in good!" he moaned.

Then, thinking of Max, he suddenly became gentler when he said:

"You want to cum, baby? You want me to let you cum?"

"Yeessss, Big Daddy," Max cried.

With his own cock still in him, Donnie took Max's cock-ring off. Turning him over so that they were on their sides on the bed, Donnie's hand pumped Max's cock while his thrusts came hard and fast. And, it didn't take long before Max, moaning and crying, exploded into Donnie's hands.

* * * *

And that was the first day. All-in-all, Donnie had taken Max three times, once before he was examined by the doctor, and once afterwards, before he sent him to pick up their sons, and again when he returned to work that evening.

It was well after midnight when Max got home. He had showered before leaving the Lodge. Now, considering what he had been through that day, he had no desire to be close to anyone. In sweats, he stretched out on the couch in the darkened living room, and closed him eyes. But he would find no sleep that night. Just as he had consumed his body that day, Donnie consumed his mind that night.

Laying there thinking, still sore and aching, he wondered what he had gotten himself into.

I'm not a homo, he thought. *At least I said that...*

Uummmm... he was rubbing himself. *Damn! Damn! It hurts so fucking good, though!*

Ah man, don't say that! Getting fucked? What are you thinking?!

I don't know... Shit! I don't know! But...that damn mutha-fucka got my ass aching. He hurt me so damn good! Sooo fuckin' good!

Ah man, that's how he wants you to feel, man... 'cause he's gonna keep on fuckin' and hurtin' your ass with that big-ass fucking dick! Man!.... Man?! Why... you mutha-fucka! You want it! You want the hurt! 'Cause you want to be fucked! You want him to hurt you! Don't you? You want him to fuck you! Don't you?! You want him to hurt you! Don't you?! You want him to fuck you! Don't you? Don't you?! Don't you?!

70

Chapter VIII

Those first weeks Max couldn't wait for the break when he would pick up Brian and Trey, usually in one of Donnie's SUVs, and take them to practice. Were it not for those breaks, no doubt he feared, Donnie would have fucked him all day long those first weeks.

Most of the times, he used the time alone turning over and over in his head, again and again, the ambivalence he felt between his mind and body. Those first weeks he could think of nothing else. He was in constant turmoil. So, when he picked up the boys, he knew he had 2 or 3 hours to himself, pretty much. Many times he would stay alone in the SUV thinking—not wanting to be with other men for fear they might know or be able to sense what he had become.

A couple of months ago, he didn't know men like Donnie Soledad Williams existed. He had been content to write his poetry, to teach and to work his plan to start a boys' club where he would coach kids, like he had coached his son. After he became Donnie's *personal assistant*, he felt that had become an impossible dream.

Those first weeks passed with Max drinking and smoking and taking anything and everything he could get his hands on to alter his consciousness enough, he told himself, so he could give himself to Donnie. And it seemed to him that if he wasn't being taken by Donnie, he was on somebody's bed, knocked out.

During those first weeks, he didn't see Pretty Boy around much anymore. When he first saw him—his beauty, his femininity—he had been certain Pretty Boy was Donnie's lover. For the life of him, he couldn't see why Donnie spent all his time doing him, and not Pretty Boy. And when he had casually mentioned Pretty Boy to Donnie one day, Donnie had said: "He's not only the prettiest sissy I've ever seen, with that sweet-ass tongue, he's got a good heart.... But, he's not my type and he ain't got what you got, baby," he said, rubbing Max's ass. "It ain't like yours.... Besides, he's volunteering at an HIV hospice across town, somewhere... don't think he's fucking anybody over there. But he's too close to that shit for me."

Still, Donnie always had a crew around to do his bidding. They bathed Max whenever he had been too out of it to bathe himself. They cleaned, oiled, shaved, waxed, massaged, exercised and purged him whenever Donnie ordered. They fed him, fondled him, and kept him feeling good, like Donnie wanted.

His days usually started around 7 in the morning. After taking Brian to school, he would go to Donnie. Sometimes, there was breakfast. Sometimes, *he* was breakfast, but there was always Donnie, who would fuck him at least once everyday before picking up their sons and taking them to practice. Then, back to spend another 4 to 6 hours at the mercy of Donnie's mercurial mental and physical nature, where he could be beaten, bitten, sucked and fucked, and sometimes turned over to any of several of his ever-changing teams of drones, for their pleasures for hours. Their only prohibition being, no one could penetrate him, anally or orally, except Donnie.

Most nights he would crawl in bed beside Kimberly a little after midnight with his head still reeling from whatever he had used to bring him through; his body satiated, sore and aching, it was easy to fall into a deeply sleep.

At first though, many times he could not snort, smoke or drink enough to stop the torment in his mind.

It would often follow him home and play out in his dreams. One dream came to him often in a series of flashes. A dream where he would find himself chained, standing naked in a damp, dark cellar. Donnie is beating him with a whip. Then, inserting the handle. *Say you want it!* Donnie demands, up close behind him. *Say you love it! I want it! I love it!* And Donnie takes it out, roughly! In the dream, he beats Max, and then inserts it! *Say you're my bitch! Say you're a ho....* Suddenly, in his dream, he realizes he really does love it–the pain, the ecstasy, being controlled. But, he always wakes with a start before he would allow himself to accept it.

One night the dream ended with Donnie, after having flogged and whip-fucked a crying Max, giving him head, and Max was enjoying it, thoroughly. Then suddenly, Max realized his cock was actually being sucked! He awoke, abruptly.

It was Kimberly.

Before that night, they hadn't made love since Donnie raped Max, and now that was over two months ago. Though she really had tried on several occasions, Max was having trouble getting and keeping it up for her. He felt it was because of what Donnie was doing to him. But he dared not tell her that. So she saw it as rejection. She was certain he was having an affair at Donnie's. He had had several in the past. But she knew she loved him. And she knew he loved Brian and would never leave them.

* * * *

As for Donnie, he was thoroughly enjoying himself with his personal assistant. For reasons beyond his comprehension, he found himself wanting Max like he had never wanted anyone else. Most mornings he was hard before Max arrived.

Most nights he found himself angry when he left. But Donnie would never let his mind dwell on anything as uncontrollable as emotions. All he wanted to entertain was the way his cock felt when it was totally inside Max's ass. All he knew was he loved that sensation, and that he would do whatever he had to do to keep on feeling it.

Still, every time Max left to go home to Brian and Kimberly, Donnie's need to possess him grew stronger. He couldn't bear the thought of Max being a man with Kimberly. For him, Max, like all the others, had to be submissive, willing and eager—and still, Max wasn't. And this fact, though he wouldn't allow his mind to entertain it, tormented Donnie.

Late one evening when he had returned from taking the boys home, Donnie came in, sat on the bed and removed his sweats. Lying back onto the pillows, rubbing his hardening cock, he looked at Max who stood staring out the window.

"You still wearing your ring?" Donnie asked, matter-of-factly. Max turned and looked at him. Donnie was still rubbing and fondling at his huge member.

Though it took a while for Max to fully accept what he had become to let Donnie do what he did to him, it didn't take long for him to get use to Donnie's money. Still, he held on to the belief that he was with Donnie only for the money and because Donnie could get Brian a major league contract. In holding on to these beliefs, as time went on and as he grew accustomed to Donnie's ways, Max became jaded.

That evening he had been thinking about how to tell Donnie he wanted out. That he didn't like what it was doing to him. But now, looking at Donnie, he was surprised at how instantly his own body was reacting to the full sight of his nakedness.

"No, I'm not wearing a ring," Max answered, tritely. Though he was already hardening from the sight of Donnie's nakedness.

Without saying anything further, he turned and went to the bureau where he found the cock-ring he liked best, and pulled his own cock through it. Then, he went to the bed where Donnie lay, and lay down beside him.

Now, Donnie saw the disgusted submissiveness in Max's face.

"Why can't I let your ass go?!" Donnie asked, seeing that look he hated in Max's eyes. The look that said all too clearly to him that, *Max doesn't want to be here. He still doesn't want me,* while tightening the cock-ring on Max.

"For the same reason I can't say no to you," Max replied, simply, and turned his back to Donnie, cuddling a pillow.

He closed his eyes and gasped loudly, as the head of Donnie's cock entered him. Breathing hard through his mouth, Max grabbed the pillow and held it tight. All you could hear was the rustling of the bed and their breathing, until Donnie had pushed himself all the way in. Now he was at Max's ear.

"Nooo... you can't say no to me!" Donnie whispered. He let his teeth sink into Max's earlobe. "I won't let you! With ass this sweet—it won't let you.... 'Cause this ass-pussy's too sweet, baby! It's the best! Your ass belongs to me!" His arms were around Max's waist. His right hand gripping and squeezing Max's balls, his left pumping his cock. "Don't you? Don't you?!"

Max heard Donnie insistence over his own sighs and moans.

"Yesss, Big Daddy!" he cried out in the grip of his erotic pain and pleasure. His body could no longer allow him to tell himself he didn't want this.

Feeling Donnie's hands commanding his pain and his huge member sliding in and out of him, commanding his ecstasy, Max knew his body would never be able to say no to Donnie. He knew his body wanted—no, at this moment he felt—needed this.

Donnie slapped his ass.

"God!" Max moaned, "I hate this...." Then, "...you hurt it so good, Big Daddy! You hurt it soooo good!"

Slapping it once more. "Tighten it up!" Donnie ordered, pushing all the way in, and holding it, while squeezing Max's balls and cock. "Squeeze it!" he demanded.

Max squeezed his gluteus maximus, tightly gripping Donnie's phallus!

Donnie felt Max's muscles tighten around him.

"Aahhhh, baby... baby!" he exclaimed, as the cum shot from him and into his compliant subject. "Fuck this dick, baby! This ass' soooo sweet! It's good, baby!" he breathlessly licked into Max's ear, letting up on his balls and cock a bit, but staying in him.

Max could feel Donnie's hot fluid filling him.

"Pleaseee," Max moaned.

In his own bliss, Donnie managed to roll Max's cock-ring off, and with his hand, he pumped Max's cock fast for a few seconds, and continued to hold onto it as his cum oozed out and flowed down onto Donnie's hand.

"Aahhhh!.... I hate it.... Aahhh... pleaseee, Big Daddy!" Max cried.

"Please, what?!" Donnie asked, curiously, as if he had never heard Max say the word before. "Fuck you some more?! Hurt your ass? What do you want me to do?"

Unsure of his tone, scared of what he might do next, Max managed to say: "Please, let me go home."

"Take your ass home!" Donnie said, angrily. Pulling out and moving away from him, he stood up. "See if you can fuck her after that!" He spat the words at Max, who lay looking at his nakedness, unsure of his sudden anger and his reference to Kimberly.

Donnie grabbed his forearm and pulled him from the bed. Donnie stood gripping Max's forearms and holding him close so that their cocks touched, forcing Max to look at him.

"Noooo... you can't fuck her!" Donnie said, in his face. "After that, your ass couldn't fuck butter!" He let Max go. "Go on, take your tired ass home, mutha-fucka!" Donnie said, pulling on his pants. "I don't need your ass!"

He left Max sitting on the bed.

* * * *

Late one evening when Donnie sat in his office counting out a wad of money for Sharon, she came around behind where he was and gently placed a tattered picture down before him.

He lost count.

He recognized the person in the picture immediately, and picked it up.

"Remind you of anyone?" Sharon asked, coming back around in front of him to see his reaction.

"No one other than who it is," Donnie said. He put the picture down, and started counting the money again, silently.

75

"Well, he reminds me of someone else," Sharon said.

This conversation took place a couple of months later. They were in Donnie's office.

"Yeah," Donnie said, quietly looking at the picture. "And, who might that be?"

The man in the picture had Donnie and Max's pecan-brown skin coloring, but he had Max's build and mustache.

"You don't see the resemblance?!" Sharon asked, picking up the picture and looking at it, closely.

"I don't see any resemblance," he said, flatly. But, it was evident he knew who it was she was talking about.

"You may not see it, baby. But, I can. And I believe that's why you've gotta have him.... That may be why I got him for you," she said, reflectively. "I mean, I knew he wanted to be fucked from the minute I laid eyes on him. And I think I saw something else in him... or... someone else."

"Don't fuck with me, Sharon! I didn't fuck him," Donnie said. His face was emotionless, though there was a bit of irritation in his voice.

"No," Sharon continued. "But, if he hadn't left maybe that other fucka wouldn't have come into your life... our lives, and fucked up everybody."

His past was one of the things Donnie didn't like to think about, but that conversation put the past front and center on his mind.

For Donnie that night when he was doing Max, making Max say how much he loved him, was not unlike those night years ago when the man he had been forced to call daddy would say those things to him. That had taken place a long time ago when his mother's husband fell in love with his huge, growing cock, and he awoke one night to find the man's mouth on him.

His mother had married this man after his father left, because she knew he could give them a good life.

Donnie owned the man after that night. And from that time on, Donnie used the one sure thing he had to own anybody who wanted to get close to him—or, anybody he wanted to get close to.

In truth, Max did look a lot like the man in the photograph Sharon had shown him. To Donnie, he acted like his stepfather—wanting it, getting it—yet trying to hold onto the straight life lie, denying to himself that he was queer. But there was no denying Donnie loved fucking Max. For a reason unknown to him, he found their sex more satisfying than anyone he had ever been with, including Sharon. And he knew Sharon had spoken the truth when she said Max wanted it too, even if he had to feel the pain so he could let himself feel the pleasure. With Max, he could get every inch of his 13" phallus inside. The more he hurt him, the more it seemed to turn them both on. And that made it all the better for Donnie. He knew he had to keep Max. He knew he had to own him. How?

* * * * *

The answer came one night as he and Max lay naked, together, their bronzed bodies steaming with sweat. Donnie had just fallen off.

It was something Trey had told him Brian said: *My Dad's the greatest coach! He's gonna open a boys' club!—and be the coach!"* The instant Donnie heard it he knew it was something he could use.

"Coaching a boys' club, huh.... Well, I'll help you get it, baby," he had said, exhaustedly, handing Max the joint he had just pulled on, and pouring himself a shot of Courvoisier.

They were in his bed, in his bedroom, a room three times the size of Max's *office*. It was lavishly furnished and decorated with dark satins and leopards.

"How can you help me? I mean, what can you do?" Max asked, almost indignantly.

Donnie chuckled. "Money talks, baby... don't you know that?"

Max knew how much the money Donnie was paying him talked. It was more money than he had ever made on any of the teaching jobs he had.

He didn't answer.

"With some grant money and, your sterling reputation.... I'll show you what I can do," Donnie continued. "If that's what you want to do, baby."

Max didn't know what to say. He felt certain Donnie could do it. And the possibility that he would help him instantly gave Max a renewed feeling of hope that he might have a chance to be something other than Donnie's personal assistant until Donnie grew tired of him.

"Would... you help me? I mean, really show me how to get in the business?" he heard himself ask.

"If that's what you want," Donnie replied, turning Max's face toward him. He had heard a longing in his voice, and it turned him on. "As long as you give me what I want." He gave Max several soft kisses, and then he sent his tongue into his mouth.

This was the first time Max took it, tasting the liquor he had been drinking and the smoke.

And this was the first time Max had given Donnie his tongue. And he would often remember how it seemed to have driven Donnie wild.

Donnie had used his tongue all over Max's body that night. Going from his mouth, Donnie's mouth first moved to his throat, sucking hard and long.

"Aaahhhhh, Big Daddy... Goddd... don't mark me," he remembered crying with a certain delight in his voice, as Donnie licked and kissed and sucked so hard, the marks were inevitable.

Sucking his breath in between his teeth, "Oohhhaahhh, Big Daddy... you hurt me so good!" Max cried, as Donnie sucked and sank his teeth into his nipples. "So good!"

Breathing hard in surrender, Max moved sensuously as Donnie licked and sucked his entire belly before ending up at his naval, licking and sucking and nibbling it.

"Aaahhhhhh! Mmmmm!" Max sighed, his head swooning with ecstasy as Donnie's mouth, starting at the head of his cock and pushing the foreskin back with his lips, engulfed it. "I'll be whatever you want, Big Daddy! I'll do whatever you want!" Max heard himself cry, surrendering to his master's every stroke.

Donnie's mouth moved effortlessly from his cock to his balls. Max's sighs and moans had become faster and louder, and he would have cum had Donnie's not used his fingers to stop his flow. "It's yours, Big Daddy! I'm yours! I'll do whatever you want me to do!" he cried out in anguish.

"Uh-huh," Donnie said as he turned him, propped his legs and laid between them. Resting his head on Max's thigh, he licked from his balls, to the base of him, to his buns and anus, licking and kissing and sucking and nibbling and biting.

"Yesss! Big Daddy! God yeesss!" Max cried. Sighing: "I'm yours! I'm yours, Big Daddy! Take it! Oh god! Oh god!!!! Fuck me, Big Daddy! Fuck me! Fuck!" Max heard himself pleading.

And Donnie heard his pleading too.

"Do you hate me now, baby?!" he murmured, while gnawing Max. "Do you hate me now?"

"Noooo…. No, Big Daddy…. I want… I want it! I want it!" Max sighed, moving his body sensuously, erotically.

Donnie brought him up onto his knees to meet his masterful, huge, plummeting rod. Resting his engorged member upon Max's buns, rubbing his ass soothingly, Donnie used his thumbs to part and open him. Then, arching his own ass back just so, his huge cock fell into Max's open anus, like it was falling into a slot. He slowly pushed it in once more, watching his cock being consumed.

"Is this my ass-pussy?!" Donnie asked, breathlessly. "Huh? Is this my ass…?"

"Oohhhh… God! Pleaseeee!" Max cried, as he entered that zone where only Donnie could take him. "It's your ass-pussy, Big Daddy! I'll be anything you want… I'm yours!"

And he was. For now he felt he had a reason to surrender to what he felt was this prurient desire.

* * * *

Donnie had known Sharon for as long as he could remember. They had been boyfriend and girlfriend all through junior high and high school. So it wasn't a surprise to anyone who knew them then when Sharon got pregnant with Donnie's son, Trey, though they had sex only that one time when he raped her.

That was the night of his rampage.

Earlier that day, his mother had driven her car across the median and crashed headlong into a pick-up truck.

In his bones he knew that she had done it deliberately to end her life. A week earlier, he had been certain he had caught a glimpse of her horrified face in the bedroom dresser mirror, as he stood on the side of their bed banging his stepfather. She never mentioned it, and neither did he. But he would remember he didn't hear her say a word to him or his stepfather that last week. It was like she was moving away from them into another world. He and Sharon were both 17.

So on that day when his stepfather gave him the news, he beat him to a bloody pulp. Then, half out of his head with guilt and grief, he went to Sharon. She had to have 12 sutures. But she loved Donnie. And, when he came to his senses, he was truly sorry for what he had done to her. She, like his stepfather, decided not to bring charges against him. Though she had to stay in bed for seven months after they found out she was pregnant.

An athlete, Donnie Williams was on his way to college. Everyone who knew him knew he would return home a rich and famous man some day. He knew it too. Although Donnie was now well off, back then he learned that his riches wouldn't come from his athletic abilities on the field.

As for Max, by now he knew Donnie wanted him. That had been something he had always been able to tell with females, and he was learning that it wasn't that much different with males. He knew Donnie had sought him out, made him, and was now paying him to let him fuck him. Yes, he knew Donnie wanted him. And now Donnie was talking about helping him with his dream. Yes, he made up his mind, he would be with Donnie if he wanted to buy him.

Maybe this could turn into something real, he thought. *Maybe I'll end up running this place!*

And that night he also decided that he would be with Donnie whenever Donnie wanted. Because when it was over that night, he could no longer deny the fact that he loved being taken the way Donnie took him.

* * * * *

A few days later Donnie, true to his word, had attorneys draft and file the proper papers. He used Max's desire for the boys' club to make him stay longer at night and to bring him in on Saturdays and Sundays, whenever he wanted him.

It was on one of those Saturdays shortly after the papers were filed, when Max received the first weekend call from Donnie telling him he was needed in the office to read over and sign some papers.

Now at Donnie's, Max hadn't been in his room reading the papers no more than 5 minutes when Donnie came in, closed and locked the door. Coming up behind Max, who stood in front of the desk with the mirror hanging over it, Donnie slipped his arms around his waist, one hand went underneath his shirt, the other inside his pants.

"I knew this was why you made me come in to look at these papers, man!" Max quipped, with mild irritation clearly in his voice.

"Mmmm, I'm glad you wore sweats, baby," Donnie said, standing behind Max, rubbing him, finding and nibbling his earlobe, as Max tried to continue reading the papers. "Let me hit it," Donnie whispered.

"No, man! Come on… my son's downstairs!" Max exclaimed, no longer able to pretend to be reading the papers.

"And we're up here," Donnie said, nibbling, while his hands massaged. "Nobody's coming in… and you ain't going nowhere! I locked the door."

Max's mind was trying to ignore Donnie's arms around him, his massaging hands, but his body was already responding. Donnie slipped two fingers into Max's anus.

"Aaahhhhh! You fucka!" Max protested mildly, tossing his head back in surrender, unable to ignore Donnie any longer.

"Bend over, baby," Donnie whispered. "I'll make it fast… a quickie!" And then he was inside Max, who stood, using the table in front of him to brace himself.

Taking it and knowing his son was in the building, Max tried to muffle the cry that escaped his throat each time Donnie pumped himself up into him.

"This my ass-pussy, baby?" Donnie asked, and slapped his bun. "This my ass-pussy?!!"

"Yesss, Big Daddy…. Yesss… it's your ass-pussy," Max moaned. Unable to resist, he was already entering the zone.

Max knew the papers he had been trying to read had come in the day before. He knew that before he left home, and he knew that this was the real reason Donnie had called and insisted he come to go over them. Still, he had come. It was happening and he was, once again, in the zone.

On their way home that day, Max stopped at a gas station and filled the tank, while Brian went inside the store for a soda. When he finished, he got back into the car. Sitting there, staring into the side-view mirror at his face. It was a face he didn't recognize much anymore. His nipples burned as he thought of the merciless way Donnie had squeezed, pinched and bitten them, and he felt his whole body go weak just from the thought.

Do I look any different? he wondered. *Can they see what he's doing to me? Does anybody else know... besides me?!*

Because, if he knew nothing else he knew that when it came to sex, he preferred the way Donnie made love to him more than the way he had ever made love to Kimberly—or, to anybody else.

God! I can't help it! I love the way it feels. But... that don't make me a fag! Some part of his brain quickly retorted. *Bi... maybe. But I'm no fag anymore than Donnie is! We just want—more... that's all!*

To the mirror, looking into his own eyes, he murmured, "I'm a man! I'm a real fuckin' man!"

"What you say, Dad?!" Brian asked, getting into the car.

"Man, it's about time!" Max recovered quickly, and lied.

He put the car in gear, and sped off toward home.

Chapter IX

By now there was no communication between Max and Kimberly. When they were together, the guilt he felt for wanting Donnie more than her was overbearing. He consoled himself with the fact that in the beginning he had tried to make it clear to her that he was with her because of their son. He had actually said as much when she insisted he move in after she told him she was pregnant. Now, he found himself purposefully avoiding her, wanting to spend more time at Donnie's. He felt she was avoiding him as well.

"I'm not having an abortion," Kimberly had said. "You should have used the condom!"

"And you was supposed to be taking birth control pills, Kim! What about that?!" Max had fired back, defensively.

"I told you the doctor took me off the pills...."

"I don't remember that! I don't remember you telling me that!"

"Well, I told you that. And I'm not having an abortion. It's murder... and I'm not doing it! I don't care what you say."

I'm not ready to get married and raise a family, Kimberly...."

"I'm not asking you to marry me! I just want you to do your part and help me take care of *your* child. That's all."

"That's all," Max repeated the words, feeling as if she was asking for his world. And even in his repeating them, he felt that was not all. He knew he would not want another man raising his son. He knew he would be bound to Kimberly forever, and he didn't like it. But he had been raised to take responsibility for his own. Though both of his parents were dead by the time Brian was born, the responsibility for his son had been ingrained. So, when Brian was born, Max dutifully moved in with his new family.

* * * *

Now, Donnie took Max, or had Max service him, at least once, but usually two or three, sometimes four times a day. And if he brought Brian to the gym on Sundays, it happened on a Sunday.

Max continued to tell himself the real reason he was with Donnie was because he wanted the boys' club. *That would be something good,* is what he told himself. So with liquor and drugs, and the pain, he continued to let Donnie and his drones have their way with him. And whenever he got any time alone, he spent it getting information on the computer and going over plans for his boys' club.

Donnie caught him doing this one evening when he came back into his room.

"You have to work on your boys' club thing on your own time, baby," he said. Removing his pants, he threw himself onto the bed. "When you're here with me you're on my time, you're my personal assistant, remember? And I want you flat on your back... or, on your belly... or, on your knees! Now, put the papers away and come here," he ordered.

"Well, when are you going to work on it?" Max asked, disgustedly, coming to where Donnie lay. "Every time we're together... it's about fucking, Donnie!" he protested mildly.

Donnie sent his hand under the robe, "Didn't I tell you I'm handling it..." he said. Then ordered: "Take this off."

Complying, Max threw his head back in anguished surrender when one of Donnie's hands cupped and squeezed his balls, while the other one tightened the cock-ring, once more.

"Mmmmm!" Max sighed. "I want this, Big Daddy!" he groaned.

"And I'll get it for you, baby.... Now, turn around," Donnie murmured as he finished. He was seated on the side of the bed now, and his eyes and attention were on the task at hand.

He was slathering Max's anus, and then the head of his own hard cock. Positioning it at the tiny, sensuous opening, he sent his arms around Max' waist, and brought him down hard onto his hungry, waiting glans.

"Oohhhh... aaahhhh! That hurt, Big Daddy... it hurts so...."

"You want me to hurt your ass, baby! You like it rough... like this!" He pulled Max further down onto his penetrating rod. "You like for me to hurt your ass.. don't you?! That's why its sooo mutha-fuckin' good with yo'ass, baby! Why I

84

love this ass!" Donnie licked into Max's ear. "It fits my dick like a mutha-fuckin' glove!"

"Oohhhh…aaahhhh!" Max moaned.

"And… you like it rough, baby!" Donnie whispered again, as he brought him all the way down.

"Aaahhhhh!" Max exhaled.

The strength in his legs gone, Max laid his head back against Donnie's shoulder, surrendering.

Donnie's legs were inside of Max's, and Max's back was to Donnie's belly.

"I'm impaling yo'ass again, baby!" He rocked himself back and forth into Max, still whispering, "All this dick's in you! That's why I love fucking yo'ass!" he said.

While keeping his massive glans buried in Max, he swung their bodies and legs around so that they lay on the bed together, side by side. With undulating hunches he took him, as Max lay sighing and moaning—surrendering—in the zone.

* * * *

After Donnie agreed to help him with the boys' club, Max was finding it harder and harder to continue denying to himself how much he wanted sex with Donnie. Though he still vacillated, especially when he was with his son. Then, it was easy for him to continue telling himself he was doing it for the money and that was what kept him coming back—the money and what Donnie could do for him and his son.

So, when school started later that year and Max was offered a permanent teaching position, he turned it down. He told himself he did it because he was making more money being Donnie's personal assistant.

His mind refused to allow him to question how long this arrangement could go on. Because, without realizing it, with Donnie he felt a type of security he hadn't felt since before his parents died. Somewhere in the back of his mind he knew he wanted that feeling, almost as much as his body wanted Donnie's body. So, he kept coming to Donnie, still refusing to totally admit to himself that he wanted to be there, in the zone where only Donnie could take him.

Though he had been able to fight the truth about his feelings in the beginning, after more than four months of being with Donnie, his ambivalence was fading. And, it was becoming harder and harder for him to deny to himself the changes taking place within.

The first time he admitted it was one morning when Donnie had him achingly in the zone. Feeling both the pain in front of him and the pleasure entering him from behind, Max had to admit that this was the feeling he couldn't resist. No one had ever made him feel like that except Donnie. At times like this, when his mind and his body were totally in the zone, the world could have ended and Max would have been oblivious to it. In fact, the world as he had known it did end in that moment, because at that moment Max had to admit that this was where he wanted to be.

"Aahhhhh! Fuck me, Big Daddy!" he lay crying in complete surrender to his ecstasy. He sent his ass back to meet its pleasure. And he did it again and again and again, as he cried: "Fuck me! Big Daddy... you hurt me soooo good! You make it hurt sooo fuckin'good, Big Daddy! You hurt me sooo good...."

"'Cause... you got the best ass, baby! You got the best aassss!" Donnie hissed, and sent his cock into Max to the hilt. Holding himself there, his left hand gripped hard onto the head of Max's cock, pushing it down while his right hand gripped hard onto his balls.

Max's body shook as if in a seizure as Donnie's cum shot hard into him.

In that moment he was sure he could see it, like the hottest fireworks shooting high into a black sky.

"My dick loves this ass, baby!" Donnie whispered as he twisted the lever on Max's cock-ring, and pumped his shaft hard and fast. "You like that, baby?! You like when I let you cum?"

"Ooohhhh yeesss.... Oh Goddd, Big Daddy!" Max cried. He was feeling his own cum racing through the opening and exploding through Donnie's fingers onto the sheets. "Whoooaaaa...." he sighed, and his body shivered in ecstasy.

And then they lay there together, cooling down.

"Huh-huh-huh!" they each said, almost simultaneously.

"Tell me you don't want to feel like that, baby!" Donnie exclaimed, reaching for the joint and firing it back up.

He was still in Max as he lit it. Exhaling, he continued:

"The body don't lie, mutha-fucka!"

He pulled away from Max. Sitting on the side of the bed, he sucked hard on the joint.

"Your fucking ass don't lie," he said, rubbing Max's bun sensuously, he sent his fingers into him where moments ago his cock had been. "This sweet ass don't lie…."

"Aaahhhh…." Max sucked in the sigh. "It's changing me, man," he moaned. "This shit's changing me! God! What are you doing to me?" he groaned.

"What this sweet ass want me to do to you, baby…." Donnie sent his fingers into him a little deeper. "I'm making you mines! I'm making you my bitch."

"I'm already your fucking bitch," Max said, unable to keep his body from moving to Donnie's fingers. "Aaahhhh! You get it whenever you want it…. Aaahhhh!" he moaned again. "You've been fucking me all day, Big Daddy…." he cried, "Aaahhhhh…."

Donnie's fingers were stoking the fire within him once again. "I'm already your fucking-ass bitch, Big Daddy…. Whooaaaahhhh!" he sighed through his teeth. "It's changing me!"

"'Cause you know you can't give up this feeling, baby! You know you can't give up the dick!" Donnie hissed, while finger-fucking Max.

"Aaahhhh…. God!" Max cried. "You're making me… a punk! Big Dad…."

"You made yourself a punk! That was your… Rubicon, baby… and… you crossed it!" Donnie said, now turning to where Max lay and giving him his whole hand! "You crossed it that day when you got drunk so you could let niggas fuck this ass!!"

"Oohhhh… noooo…. Mutha-fuck! Don't…." Max said angrily, not wanting to hear what deep down he knew was the truth. He was trying to move away from Donnie hand-fucking him. But, he was too late.

Donnie had hold of him around his waist, his hand was gripping his balls, tight, while his hand was still in Max's ass. Suddenly Donnie made a fist and rammed it into Max, holding it there!

Max's body stiffened. "Ooohhhaaaahhhhh!!!" he moaned.

"Where you gonna go? Huh?!" Donnie hissed.

Letting up, Max lay still, surrendering to Donnie's fist.

"You made yourself a punk-ass, ass-pussy ho when you gave up the pussy for the moolah, baby! Besides... anybody who took what your ass took at the Lodge has gotta like it! Otherwise, you never would have gone all the way through with this shit!" Donnie continued talking while listening to the wet sound, Max's sobs as he lay there surrendering, and, enjoying the hot, slick stickiness his fist felt as he sent it in-and-out of Max—like a kid playing with a favorite toy.

* * * * *

Even after deciding to give himself to Donnie, still oftentimes it amazed him at how completely Donnie consumed his mind and his body. Even when he was at home with Brian and Kimberly, he could think about Donnie and feel himself getting hot and hard to the point that he didn't want them to see what was happening to him. He could feel himself pulling away from them. He hated it, and he hated himself for the ambivalence that constantly plagued his mind.

So one morning when Donnie was in the saddle taking Max again on the kitchen floor, his question took Max by surprise.

"Did you fuck her last night, baby? Huh? Could you fuck her?!" Donnie asked, with a sarcastic anguish clearly in his voice.

This was the first time he had ever questioned Max about his relationship with Kimberly. And Max didn't know what to say. He could say very little anyway, because Donnie was taunting him with his huge, hard cock—slapping his ass with it and his hands, plunging it deep into him, then abruptly pulling out, while squeezing and twisting his balls with one hand and his nipples with the other.

"Nooo... you can't fuck her...." he said, and slapped Max's bun. "Not after I'm done with your ass! You couldn't fuck butter, mutha-fucka!"

"Pleaseeee, Big Daddy," Max murmured. "It's doing something to me! *You're* doing something to me... Big Daddy!" Max cried, through his torment.

"Yeah... I'm hurting your ass! I mean, that's what it's going to take! I'm gonna have to hurt your ass so bad, you won't be able to go back to her!" Donnie threatened while twisting Max's balls tighter than he had ever done before!

Max groaned. "Oohhhh Godddd!" he cried. "It's changing me! Big Daddy... I... I...."

"Damn right," Donnie hissed. "Because you want the dick, bitch! Not the money... it ain't the money with you... it's the fuckin' pain – and how good this dick can make you feel! That's why you keep coming back!" he growled, slapped Max's ass and rammed his cock deep into him. Holding it there, he continued: "If you didn't... you'd walk away! You'd say fuck this shit, Big Daddy! Mutha-fucka, and you'd walk away... and get a fucking 9 to 5 like all the rest of you bitch-ass niggas do!"

"Pleaseee, Big Daddy! Don't.... I hate it!—I—I hate you! Stop pleaseee ..." Max begged, not wanting to hear the truth of the words. "I hate it!"

"You don't hate it, baby.... No nigga's gonna let a big dick fucka like me fuck you in your ass... ever-y-day... if you didn't want the dick! You love it... don't you?!" He plunged hard into Max.

It was the truth of Donnie's words that hurt him. Yet, it was then, when hearing the truth of the words that Max knew he couldn't deny it. Wanting him to stop– not wanting him to stop—he lay there taking the abuse.

"But... you can't do that, either!" Donnie said, his voice filled with a sarcastic anguish. "You can't... you won't walk away, will you?! Because you're a selfish..." he slapped Max loud and hard, "... ass-pussy ho... ain't you?!" he asked, and rammed himself all the way into Max again. "Answer me!" he demanded.

"Aaahhhh!.... Yesss, Big Daddy...." Max moaned in his tormented, erotic abandonment.

It was in that moment that he knew what Donnie was saying was true. He realized he had cross his Rubicon the moment he had gone back to Sharon's to be fucked by men. He knew he had gone there, because something in him wanted it. He had gone to the Lodge for the same reason. And, he knew he would keep coming back to Donnie. Because now, Donnie had placed Max's legs over each shoulder, and was taking him face-on, full-throttle! It was the way Max liked most. So, he gave himself over to the ecstasy and the agony of his deliriously delicious torment—totally.

"It's your ass-pussy! It's yours... Big Daddy! F-u-c-k!!!" he cried once again in absolute ecstasy.

"Then... it's got to be mine's!" Donnie rammed himself into him once more. Then, pulled out and came so powerfully it landed on Max's chin, chest and stomach. "Uh-uh-uh!" he moaned. "I own this ass-pussy, baby!" he fell to the bed bedside Max.

Max, feeling triumphant that Donnie had let his guard down, turned and tried to remove the cock-ring, but Donnie took hold of his wrists stopping him.

"Not yet, baby! I'm not done with your ass, yet," he said.

Chapter X

One morning about a week or so later, Donnie left almost as soon as Max arrived. He had left several times before like this, and Max assumed like he did the others times that it probably had something to do with the Lodge. So he had time alone. Not wanting to lie around thinking, he worked out in the gym and spent time alone in the sauna. His status had changed around the Lodge, and he no longer had to contend with Donnie's crew if he didn't want to.

Before he left, Donnie told Max he would pick the boys up from school that afternoon. So Max was pleasantly surprised to find Pretty Boy in his room when he returned. His workout had gone well. The sauna had soothed him right out, and he thought, *Here's a little Pretty Boy just in time to finish the job!*

Pretty Boy was at the bar.

"Make me one," Max said, using his towel to slap him on the behind before falling across the bed, wearing only a short, black satin robe.

Pretty Boy had already made a concoction for Max; he stirred it, thoroughly now. Then, he brought it to him.

"Donnie told me to keep you company 'til he gets back," Pretty Boy said, sitting on the bed beside him. "What shall we drink to?" he asked almost playfully gay.

"Why don't we drink to that *tongue* of yours," Max said, and turned up his drink.

Pretty Boy licked his lips slowly, taking his tongue across the top one, then the bottom one, sensuously. He turned his drink up. Then, he untied Max's robe.

"Uh-huh...uh-huh... I see," Pretty Boy said, putting his glass down, "I can see how he's been working on this stuff!...." he exclaimed. "Really working on these balls, baby!"

Max immediately closed the flap on his robe, re-covering himself.

"Uh-uh, man-child in the promise land!" Pretty Boy chided, opening the flap again, almost in the same motion. "Don't be covering them up. I guess you know by now, from the look of these here, he's got a thing going on with big nuts... and big tits," he said, caressing his own large breasts. His other hand was caressing Max's balls. "He wants big nuts almost as much as he wants big tits. Besides, he told me to suck out all that hurt he's been putting on these, baby. Uhh-uhh-uhh, I can sure see how hard he's been working on 'em!"

And with that, Pretty Boy put Max's penis up onto his belly and held it there as he slowly poured the rest of his drink over Max's breasts, stomach, cock, and swollen balls. Slowly, taking long, sucking licks, he lapped up all the liquid. Then, he took both his balls in his mouth and sucked.

"Whooaahhh! Man! That feels soooo…damn… good!" Max declared. He fell back on his arms and elbows, and closed his eyes. His moans filled the air as Pretty Boy's long, knowledgeable tongue, his mouth, and his teeth left no part of Max unexplored.

And, if there had ever been any question in Max's mind, Pretty Boy was making it clear to him why Donnie kept him around.

With his eyes closed, Max's head went down to the bed, lost in the ecstasy of Pretty Boy's technique and gloriously hot, wet mouth. He didn't want to think of anything or anyone. He only wanted to feel the sheer pleasures of the *master oraller!*

He had no idea his son was in the building.

Brian noticed the door to his dad's office was ajar. As soon as he heard the sounds, the boy felt apprehensive. He had heard similar sounds before, once when he opened his parents' bedroom door without knocking. He found his dad naked, on top of his mother. They both laughed sheepishly, and went under the sheets when they realized he was in the room. He had been too young to suspect anything, then. But now, he was old enough to know what those sounds meant, and he knew his mother wasn't here. Slowly, quietly, he pushed the door open, and stared!

Shocked! Backing up, Brian bumped the door.

Again Max was too erotically-consumed to see, his moans too loud to hear. But when Brian's eyes met Pretty Boy's, who stared at him with a devilish smile on his face, licking his lips, Brian ran away!

"Mmmm… what's that?" Max murmured, lifting his head slightly, as Pretty boy's lips came up to his nipples, licking, kissing and sucking, and pushing him back down on the bed.

"The wind got the door, baby… that's all," murmuring, he lied while licking Max's belly, and taking his lips down and around the head of Max's cock, he started sucking it like he was sucking a lollipop.

Max threw his head back and drew his breath in between his teeth.

"Aahhhhh..." he moaned as Pretty Boy pulled his cock back between his balls and sucked it. Then, turning him over, Pretty Boy rimmed, licked, grasped and sucked hard on his anus. Max's cum shot into the air, and landed on his own ass.

Mission accomplished, on his knees between Max's legs, Pretty Boy massaged Max's cum into his buns with both hands, going around, and around, and around.

* * * *

As Donnie was coming into the building, Brian bumped into him as he tried to run out.

"I want to go home! Can you take me home?!" the boy cried.

"Whoa! Go home? I just parked the car! Where's Trey? I thought you guys...." Then Donnie noticed Brian was crying. "What's wrong? Where's your dad?!" Donnie asked, taking Brian by the shoulders.

"Ah... I don't know!" Brian cried. "I just want to go home! Please take me home!"

"Okay! Okay! Come on. You want Trey to come with us?" Donnie asked.

"No, no," Brian cried. "I just need to go home!"

"Okay! I'll take you home, if you promise to tell me what happened. Did anybody hurt you?" Donnie's voice was sincere.

"No. Take me home!"

"All right. Come on." Donnie led him to his car, and he drove Brian home. He was feeling triumphant, with just a tinge of regret for the boy.

* * * *

If Max had noticed he would have seen the 24-hour locksmith truck that passed him when he entered the subdivision, and that there was stuff on the front lawn. But it was late and as usual after leaving Donnie's, he wasn't noticing much of anything. It was the day he forgot his key, and the garage door was locked, so he had to get out of the car and unlock the door. Fumbling, he was grateful for the moonlight until he realized he had put the right key in the door. It just wasn't

93

turning. He headed for the front. Placing what he knew was the right key in the lock, he was dumbfounded when the key wouldn't turn in that door either. He stepped back into the moonlight at the end of the stoop. Then he realized what he had seen on the lawn. Turning slowly, it all began to click when he saw his personal belongings piled, haphazardly, in the yard. He stepped out onto the lawn and looked up at their bedroom window. He saw her.

"Open the door, Kimberly," he said in a voice loud enough for her to hear him.

"You don't live here anymore," Kimberly replied. He could tell by her voice that she had been crying; and, that she was serious.

"What the hell are you talking about?! What's this all about?!" Max almost yelled. "Open the god-damn door!"

"No!" Kimberly said. "I don't want you here... and your son don't want you here either, Max! How could you let him see you?! How could you let him see that?!"

Shocked, instantly Max knew that Brian must have seen him and Pretty Boy. The events of the day flashed through his head, and he knew who had been at his office door when he and Pretty Boy had been together. He could say nothing more.

He didn't know how he had gotten back into his car, or how he had driven back to Donnie's. All he could think about was getting his hands on something to dull the massive pain he felt in his gut, and to stop the trembles. He hit four rows of cocaine Donnie kept in his room before he fell back on the bed, and cried.

He hated himself. He hated Kimberly. But most of all, he hated Pretty Boy, Donnie, and the whole sordid ring he had gotten involved with.

But it was Donnie who was beside him now, caressing him, and handing him a drink.

"Get the fuck away from me," Max said coldly, refusing the drink.

"First Brian... now, you! What the fuck's going on?!" Donnie asked feigning ignorance and innocence.

"You did this!" Max said, getting up from the bed.

Donnie took a swallow of his drink. "I don't know what the fuck you're talking about," he said, standing and innocently heading toward the door. Before opening it he turned to Max, who had been angrily watching him. "But, when I took Brian home, he said he wants to go to the Academy with Trey…."

"Youuu fucking-ass bastard!!" Max growled, lunging at Donnie, pushing him into the door and sending the glass shattering to the floor. His hands were at Donnie's throat. "You set me up! You sent that fag in here! And you sent my boy!" Max cried, as Donnie's fists and arms came underneath his grip, and with a powerful shove, sent Max flying across the room.

Max hit the wall and fell to the floor.

Now Donnie was on him, pinning him face down as Max scuffled.

"You crazy-ass, bitch!!" Donnie hissed. "You come to me like this?! Over some shit between you and your bitch, bitch?!" he said, bewildered, with an anger in his voice like none Max had ever heard.

His knee was in Max's back. He had hold of his right arm, clamping it back, and blindly fumbling through a drawer in a nearby chest as Max scuffled. "She mad because you can't fuck her?! Huh?! Huh?!"

Then his hand found what it was fumbling for. It came out with a huge, black, rubber dildo.

"Nooo!" Max cried and tried to scuttle away as the first blow landed hard on his back! "God! Nooo… you bastard!" he cried. He managed to scamper into a corner with his hands out trying to protect himself, when the next blow landed on his shoulder, and then his arm, and then the side of his head.

"Oh no, mutha-fucka! Don't stop, now!" Donnie said, grasping his wrists, and dragging him into the center of the room, toward the bed. Another blow from the dildo caught him on his ass and prostrated him. "You come here to kick my ass 'cause you let your son catch you and Pretty Boy fucking around, mutha-fucka?!" He landed another blow on his ass, and pushed him further across the floor. "When I wasn't even in the god-damn building?!" Another blow caught him.

"Nooo!" Max cried. "I hate your ass! You set me up! You bastard!"

"You bitch!" Donnie retorted with another strike. "I wasn't in the mutha-fucking building!"

"My son knows what you've done to me!" was all Max could cry. "He knows…."

He was no longer able to fight. He just lay there on the floor, sobbing, taking the beating, as Donnie found the opening he sought and painfully forced the humongous dildo into it.

But Max's mental anguish made the physical pain Donnie was inflicting on him all the sweeter—his humiliation all the more complete.

"Oohhhh!! You dog!" Max cried. "Oohhhh… I hate you! Oohhh-aaahhhh! I hate you…."

"Hate this, Mutha-fucka... hate this!!" Donnie growled, shoving the dildo deeper. In an anger-induced haze, he was ramming the dildo into Max ferociously, again and again. He didn't let up until his hands were wet from Max's natural juices, and his blood.

Like it had done when he had taken Pretty Boy, blood still freaked Donnie out. He left the dildo in Max, as he backed away, staring at the blood on his hands.

Injured and unconscious, Max lay face down. He didn't move.

* * * *

"What were you trying to do? Split his ass in two?! And give him a concussion on top of it, with that damn… weapon?!" Dr. Stewart was saying to Donnie, who sat behind the desk in his office with his elbows resting on it, his forehead buried in his palms, and his eyes closed. It was four o'clock the next morning, and Pretty Boy stood behind Donnie, massaging his shoulders.

"It was a fight," he said in defense, not looking up at the doctor, or at Melvin when he came into the room, removing a blood-stained scrubs jacket. "Is he gonna be all right?" Donnie asked.

The concern in his voice was real though possibly only Pretty Boy heard it, and it made him move away.

It was the same concern he had heard in Donnie's voice years ago when he raped him. Only this time he felt it was more intense. He sat on the couch and crossed his legs away from Donnie, listening to the conversation.

"Yeah man, in time," the Doctor said. "I gave him a sedative." He was taking something from his pocket and moving to where Donnie sat, he handed it to him. "Is that what you want?" he asked.

"How long will it take?" Donnie asked.

"How long will what take," the doctor asked.

"Before...."

"A week... maybe two.... He needed a couple of suture He needs rest... and no sex! Certainly not that rough stuff for a while, Soledad. Anyway, that shouldn't be a problem, since you'll be at the Lodge for the next few days," he concluded.

Donnie opened the desk drawer and removed a large checkbook.

"How much?" he asked, now looking up at Dr. Stewart.

"Fifteen.... He needs to take 4 a day, two in the morning and two at night."

"I want you to look in on him until I get back," Donnie said, writing a check.

"Melvin's here to see to that," Dr. Stewart said, taking the check and looking at it, pleasingly. "Most of the time, he'll sleep like a baby," Then, folding the check and putting it into the inside breast pocket of his jacket, he added: "I'll stop by tomorrow and check on him."

Chapter XI

On the stage at the Lodge all three of the triplets lay naked, face down, straps around their waists held them on slant-boards. Each one's white ass was gleaming, having already been well lubed in preparation. Each one had his own masked master who knelt in front of him facing the robed, masked and painted audience who gathered around the stage in anticipation with drinks and smokes in hand—though the big screens provided a much better view, they wanted to see the real thing. Then Soledad walked onto the stage, and excited murmurs filled the auditorium.

His white robe was removed by one member of his entourage to reveal his bronze, 6'3", well-proportioned, lean, yet muscular, naked body. Relaxed, his manhood hung down 9 inches. As he stood before the audience, two members of his entourage began slathering and massaging his hands and arms with lubricant, as Pretty Boy the final member, knelt before him. Without touching it, taking Soledad's hanging cock into his mouth, Pretty Boy wrapped his arms around Soledad's thighs and, leaning his back down to the floor, he brought Soledad down to his knees with him without dislodging the rapidly-extending glans.

The audience applauded watching Donnie Soledad Williams' great cock slide effortlessly down Pretty Boy's throat, like a man consuming a large snake, until it reached its full length. All the while, Soledad's head was back. His eyes were closed. He had to fight to put thoughts of Max out of his mind. He knew that with Pretty Boy's help he could do it.

His heavy breathing and the size of his cock signaled to the audience that he was ready. He turned, and was guided to the triplets.

Kneeling on the mat between the legs of the middle triplet, he guided the head of his hard cock into his waiting anus.

The audience gasped with excitement!

The middle triplet's ass trembled, and he let a feminine-sounding cry with each thrust.

Once he was halfway in him, Soledad's fingers began fondling the anus of the triplet on each side of him. Then, bringing his fingers and thumbs together just so, he sent his hands into each one, simultaneously.

He got his rhythm .

The triplets' sighs and moans were accompanied by contortions of their pretty faces, as Soledad's massive cock sank deeper and deeper into the middle one, and his hands and then his wrists disappeared deeper and deeper into the two on each side. And when they were in as far as they could go, over half of his cock and his forearms had disappeared inside.

The excitement of the audience and everyone on the stage was electric! Each masters' cock was hard and dripping as they eagerly watched the assaults, while working to soothe their slaves, and themselves.

Donnie Soledad Williams's cock and fists were plunging into the triplets in a rhythmic unison. His body had taken control of him now. He closed his eyes and let himself go! He was on—automatic!

The audience's squeals and edginess egged him on.

"Deeper!"

"Fifty-one!"

"Deeper!"

"Get that ass, baby!"

"Fifty-three!"

"Yeah! Ram'em good!"

He could hear some of them yelling. He could feel the insides of the triplets giving in to his plunges. His body was moving like the sex machine it had become.

"Sixty! Sixty-one! Sixty-two! "Sixty-three...."

But when his mind realized his audience was counting off, he remembered the last time he had heard them counting, and suddenly in his mind he was plunging into Max. As if awakening from a dream, Donnie Soledad Williams plunged into the triplets as deep as his fists and his cock could go, and his body shook as if in a spasm. He pulled out, violently, and the cum shot from him in powerful spurts that flew out toward the screaming audience and reached to the end of the stage.

* * * *

99

A few nights later, Donnie sat in the darkened room with a drink in his hand, watching Max sleep, and listening to him breathe. He was more than disgusted with himself for letting Max fill his mind so completely. And, no matter how hard he tried to put him out of it, he knew he was losing the battle.

He took a sip from his drink, and Max stirred a bit, turning onto his back and he lay with his bare right arm up over his head. Donnie was determined not to take him. Though Melvin had assured him Max was well-sedated and probably wouldn't even feel him, Dr. Stewart had examined him earlier when they first returned from the Lodge, and said he needed a little more time.

Donnie was determined to get what he wanted. And if somebody was in the way, it didn't matter to him if they got hurt. Now, he was determined to own Max.

That night he sat there going over in his head the conversation he had had with Kimberly about Max, as they drove back from Hargrove's Boys Boarding School.

When she asked him "I know you know where Max is, Donnie."

He readily lied, saying:

"No, I don't know, Kimberly. And, even if I did, I don't know if I could tell you. I mean... I make it a point not to get that personal with my people." Adding, "Max's a good man—he must be going through something. He told me he needed some space—would probably be gone a day or so. That was 4 days ago."

"Who did he go with, Donnie?" Kimberly insisted. "I know you know who he's seeing."

He didn't feel bad when he lied to her about Max's where-a-bouts. He didn't feel bad about lying to her about the person their son had seen him with. In fact, he felt good that Brian had told his mother about it. It worked in his favor, he thought, because now Max couldn't go home, again.

He set the glass on the table and stood up, thinking: *It's all working in my favor.* He moved to the bed and sat on the side of it, facing Max. He lifted the sheet, and ran his hand over Max's right nipple that, to him, seemed to harden under his fingers. He smiled.

"Months, huh?" he uttered, quietly.

He let the sheet fall back down over him.

Finishing his drink, Donnie left the room gently closing the door behind him, to join the triplets who had followed him back from the Lodge. They were new to the circuit, and were proving to be a fun bunch.

"Everybody wanna git with you, Soledad," they told him.

So, when they begged him to let them come to be with him, if only for a little while, he acquiesced. And in that short period of time he had already made a lot of money from their streams and DVDs. And though they could take his mind off Max, it was never for very long. Because, his mind and his heart were with Max, no matter how hard he fought it.

Since the fight, he would only allow himself to see and be near him at night, while he slept. For the first two more nights, he would steal into his room to be alone with him, and think. But on that third night, he could take it no longer.

That night he stood at the door of the darkened room for a few seconds so his eyes could adjust before moving to the bed where Max lay, in a fetal position, deep in a medical, drug-induced sleep. He didn't move when Donnie lifted the sheet and slid his naked body in next to him.

Donnie didn't want to awaken him, but lying there close to him, smelling him, he felt himself growing hard. Carefully, he sent his arm beneath Max so that his hand found him, soft and warm. Donnie's hand cupped the softness, caressing and squeezing until Max's body began to react—though he could not. Hard now, breathing hard on Max's neck, Donnie used his own wetness to rim and lubricate him, and the huge head of his own throbbing cock.

And then, he sent it in!

It seemed to force the breath out of Max, who turned his head as if he would turn over. But, unable to do so, "Mmmm," he sighed, and his head fell back onto the pillow.

Donnie didn't know whether or not he was hurting him. This time he was being gentle, he didn't want to hurt him. But he knew he couldn't stop—even if he was. He forced the breath out of Max with each thrust that took him deeper into his paradise, until he was where he wanted to be. Every inch of him had disappeared inside! On their sides, with his arms around the unconscious Max, Donnie gently rocked them both, back and forth as if putting him to sleep—until, sucking hard on the back of Max's neck, he exploded deep inside.

And then he lay still, inside his paradise.

When Max opened his eyes the next morning, he felt better than he had felt since the beating. In bed alone, he stretched, and he was surprised at how good he felt.

Doc really knows what he's doing, he thought, recalling the beating, but unaware that Donnie had left his bed only hours before.

Now, he wanted to see Donnie. He felt the need to tell him that he had been wrong by accusing him of setting him up, and that he didn't hate him. In fact, lying there, feeling good and thinking about Donnie, for the first time he realized that he wanted to be there with Donnie.

If Donnie had stayed there, maybe he would have seen these feelings on Max's face—in his body. But Donnie had awakened in a start, and quickly and quietly left, not wanting to see the anger and hate he had last seen on Max's face. He had tried to resist being with Max, he didn't want to desire him the way he did. But, if the truth be told, there had been no other absolute satisfaction for Donnie since that first night at the Lodge with Max. So he had left and gone back to his own bedroom where the triplets had been sleeping.

Now the four of them lie naked, eating breakfast on trays that had been wheeled in on a cart.

Max wanted to see Donnie. He felt he could make everything right again. He showered and hurriedly slipped into clean sweats.

Max stepped into the hall, surprising Pretty Boy who quickly stepped into the shadows, unseen and unheard. Smelling breakfast, first he went into the kitchen looking for Donnie. Then he turned and went into Donnie's bedroom—and, stopped in his tracks!

Looking at Donnie, naked, surrounded by the naked, tanned triplets, Max actually didn't know what he was experiencing. He had never truly felt pure, raw, unadulterated jealousy before, so he really didn't realize that that was what he was feeling.

"Aahhhh Max!" Donnie said, trying to cover his surprise at seeing him standing there. "Com'on in and let me introduce you to the triplets!"

"I don't think so," Max said, suddenly disgusted and angered at seeing Donnie with them all laying there glaring at him.

He didn't know Donnie had brought them back from the Lodge. When he awakened, it never occurred to him that Donnie would be in bed with someone, not to mention, with three. He was surprised, and he was angry. Though, he didn't realize why.

"But they're such sweet things..." Donnie started, "...or, should I say, they've got such sweet things, and they've been dying to meet you."

"Do they know what you do to sweet, young things like them?!" Max's voice was stealthy, cutting Donnie off. "Do they know that you drug and beat and rape sweet young things like them... or even old ass niggas like me?! 'Cause you're a fuckin' freak!" He spat the words at Donnie.

Donnie was shocked. "I think you'd better leave," he said, struggling to keep his voice even, while glaring at Max.

"Oh... I see, they're the types who like getting fucked in the ass by that big ass dick of yours, huh?!"

"Get the fuck out of here, Max!" Donnie yelled. "Take your ass back to that bitch of yours!"

"Don't you worry! I'm going... " Max was backing out the door. "To her!" he added, "Because, I'm a man! A real fuckin'man!" He slammed the door close and left.

If he wanted to cut Donnie to the bone, his words did.

"Leave... leave me! Leave me!" Donnie stammered to the surprised triplets when Max was gone. And the triplets scurried off.

Pretty Boy watched as the naked triplets scampered from the room. When they were gone, he entered and quietly closed the door. Looking at Donnie, he lightly leaned his back against it.

"Let him go, Donnie..." he whispered, "...you don't need him. Don't let him fuck with your head...."

Donnie lay on his back on the bed, naked, staring up at the ceiling. He hadn't known how Max would feel after what had happened. Now, after what he had just said, and seeing the anger in his face, Donnie felt he may have lost him. And, Donnie hated to lose.

Glaring at Pretty Boy without saying a word, he grabbed his robe from the foot of the bed and went out to the balcony, donning it.

Max had stumbled down the back stairs while fumbling for his car keys. Still, he had no idea what had made him suddenly so angry at seeing Donnie with the triplets. He thought it was because while he lay hurting, Donnie had been enjoying himself. Then the beating he had taken flashed through his mind. Anger made his hand tremble while putting the key in the ignition. When he started the car, he stopped momentarily to collect himself, resting his arms atop of the steering wheel, he rested his head on them for an instant.

Suddenly, he looked up at the balcony to Donnie's bedroom, and there he was. Max saw Donnie standing there on the balcony, his hands crammed into the pockets of his robe, peering down at him.

He peeled off!

Chapter XII

"My God, Max!" Where have you been?!" Kimberly asked, in tears as she opened the door to let him in.

Max hadn't known what to expect from Kimberly. He really hadn't planned on coming to her when he awakened that morning. But now, seeing the tears and hearing the pain and concern in her voice, he felt coming home was the right thing.

Wringing her hands, she backed into the room.

"Where were you?" she repeated. "Donnie couldn't find you. No one could!"

"Kim," Max said, coming to her, taking her hands to still them. "I'm so sorry... and ashamed," he said.

She could see in his eyes that he really meant it.

"Were you with her?" she cried, pleadingly.

Hearing Kimberly say *her* confused Max, and his face registered it.

"The 'pretty lady' Brian saw doing that to you? Donnie said he fired her."

Suddenly he understood *who* Kimberly was talking about. He realized that Brian must have mistaken Pretty Boy for a woman, and that Donnie hadn't bothered to correct him. And with that realization—knowing his manhood wasn't being questioned—he felt a shameful load being lifted from him.

"Were you with her?!" Kimberly demanded.

"Nooo! Nooo, baby!" Max said, "I just needed to go somewhere where I could think... where I could try to get my head on straight!" Max was pacing now, rubbing his head between his hands, as if to squeeze out an answer. Turning to her, "I had to get my courage up so I could talk to you—to my son! Explain to him what that was all about. And...."

"And what *was* it all about, Max?" Kimberly sobbed. "How could you let him see that?!"

105

"You won't do it!" Max retorted, accusingly. "For God's sake, Kim, I was getting a massage! We just got carried away.... I didn't even know Brian was gonna come in! I didn't know he was in the building!"

Then, while talking about Brian, Max suddenly realized he hadn't seen him.

"Where... where is he? Where's Brian?" he asked.

Kimberly looked at him with compassion. "You don't know do you?" she said, sitting down. "He doesn't was to see you, Max. He said he didn't want to be your son anymore." She said and felt a tinge of satisfaction in telling him that.

Max was speechless.

"He decided he wanted to go to boarding school after all," she continued. "Donnie took care of everything. Hargrove's, with his son. We drove him up a couple of days ago... on Thursday...."

Now Max sat down next to her on the sofa, as if her words had taken all his strength. The look on his face caused her to stop talking. She had never seen such sorrow in his face. Suddenly, compassion returned and she wanted to embrace him.

And then his tears came, and she did.

He had no desire to make love to Kimberly that night—that night filled with his tears and silent self-admonitions. It was not until morning that, half asleep, he felt her hot mouth. He let her crawl onto him, straddling. He let her guide him in, all the while silently wishing it was the other way around—silently wishing it was Donnie.

As he felt her body moving on him, he wondered had he dreamed of Donnie entering him only 24 hours ago. Thinking of him, a single tear rolled down the side of his face, and he came.

"I love you," he whispered. He didn't know whether he was saying it to her or to him.

Late the next morning after Kimberly had gone to work, Max still lie in bed staring up at the ceiling, thinking. Even in his hurt and shame at Kimberly telling him Brian didn't want to be his son anymore, he still couldn't stop thinking about Donnie.

Damn! He gets every fucking thing he wants! he thought when he felt the stir within his groin once again. A stir so powerful he had to touch himself. "Damn!" he said, sitting up when he could manage, rubbing his face in his hands.

"Why am I feeling like this?!" he cried aloud. *My son's gone. I'm no pun!... queer!... God! I love Kimberly...but... I don't... want Kimberly... I... want him!* "I hate it!" *I love it!* "Oh Goddd! What am I gonna do?!" he asked, pleadingly.

In his torment, he felt paralyzed. He didn't want to think. In that instant, he didn't want to be. *I can't take this!.... I can't take it!*

He threw the cover back and went naked into the bathroom. Searching the medicine cabinet, he found what he was looking for. He took a razor from the pack, and set it on the side of the bathtub. Then he turned on the water, and got in. He sat in the tub as the water came up around him, holding the blade to his wrists, trying to bring his mind to the deed he felt had to be done.

Why did you do this to me?! Why did you make me want it like this?!

The feeling in his groin had become more intense, his nipples hard and puckered. He put the razor down, turned the water off, and lay back, feeling the blood course through him. His hands, moving fast on his manhood, splashed water onto the floor.

"Don-nie! Don-nie!!" he cried out *his* name this time when he came.

Afterwards, lying back, relaxed, he knew what he had to do. He picked up the razor, and threw it into the trashcan.

Chapter XIII

Late that afternoon back at Donnie's Place, Max had been sitting at the bar. He stood up, anxiously, when he heard Donnie coming down the stairs. He and the bartender had been the only ones in the bar.

When he first got there, he had started up the stairs, but the bartender stopped him.

"He wants you to wait here," the bartender said, while picking up the phone. "He's here," he said.

Max came to the bar.

"Bloody Mary," he said.

"Bloody Mary it is," the bartender said, placing the drink before him.

Max turned it up.

He didn't know whether anything was in the drink. He didn't care. He just knew he had to be there—with Donnie.

He had gotten out of the bathtub and made the telephone call while he was still wet. He was surprised when Donnie wouldn't talk to him.

"Tell him I'm calling about my money," Max had lied. "He owes me!"

"He said he's mailing you a check today," chimed the chipper voice on the other end.

"Who *is* this?!" Max insisted.

"His new *personal assistant*," came the response.

"The mutha-fuckin' hell you are!" Max swore before he realized it. "Tell him I'm coming to get my fucking money!" he said, and hung up the phone before any response.

He didn't telephone Kimberly, nor did he leave her a note.

He had come back to Donnie.

He downed a second Bloody Mary before Donnie came down the steps. Now he saw him standing there, tall, lean, with muscles ripping beneath his sweats. The triplets he saw naked in his bed with him the day before were with him, and now they were dressed identically. They were laughing happily, cutting their eyes at him and talking too low for Max to hear. But he could see Donnie give each one money, and hear them squeal in delight, and kiss him in turn. Donnie slapped the last one's ass as they left.

"We love you, Big Daddy," they turned and said simultaneously, arrogantly, as they passed Max, all eyeing him with contempt.

Now Max could feel Donnie's eyes on him, and without saying a word, Donnie motioned for him to follow him into his office.

Donnie sat at his desk, leaning back in his chair with his hands clasped behind his head, he sat looking at Max.

Humbly, submissively, "What do you want me to say, man? I'm sorry... I apologize? I was mad... upset.... I mean, Kim had put me out, and you... you.... I was confused...."

"Confused?! Yeah, that's what you are mutha-fucka," Donnie said, flatly. "I hope you aren't *confused* anymore."

Sitting forward and taking his hands down, he took a check from the desk drawer and placed it on the desk.

Staring at Max, he slid the check to the end of the desk towards him, and said: "When you telephoned, this is what you told my PA I owe you for pass services. And I don't want to owe you a mutha-fuckin' thing! I had them cut the check."

This time Donnie chose words to cut Max to the bone.

Max didn't move. He didn't know what to say. He hadn't thought about what he would say when he got back there. He just knew he had to get back. Now, he couldn't make his hand reach for the check.

Seeing this and the pain in Max's face, Donnie went to the bar and made them both drinks.

Bringing the drink back to Max, Donnie saw that he had moved to the leather couch , sitting there with his face in his hand.

Sitting down beside him, Donnie handed Max his bloody Mary, and they both drank in silence.

"I'd say you've got some decisions to make, baby," Donnie said, finishing his drink. "You know you love the dick. Don't you. You know how much you love having this big hard dick in you," he was rubbing Max's back now, caressing him. "I'd say you've got to stop letting it fuck with your head. You've got to decide whether you want what I can give you, or not. It's that simple," Donnie continued. "Because I don't want you, if you don't want to be here, baby. I can't love you like you're mine, if I can't get what I need, when I need it, from you." He was whispering, close to Max's face now. "You see, I want it all... everything you've got to give, mutha-fucka.... I want that crème de la crème!" He was licking it into Max's ear, "I want to get what you've got when you think you don't have anything else to give, baby. And... I know how to get it.... And, I'm gonna get it."

Realizing from his breathing that Max wanted him to go ahead and take him, he moved away from him instead. Toying with him, he took a cock-ring from his pocket and placed it on the table in front of the couch. Then he moved to the bar, refreshing their drinks.

"But, I won't take it from you again, baby," he said from across the room with his back to Max. "You've got to want it... you've got to want me to have it... you've got to want to give it to me."

It was more than Max could take. He was hard and breathing hard now. He knew why he had come. Without saying a word, he stood and removed the sweats he was wearing, revealing the rock hard cock his pants could barely conceal. He picked up the cock-ring and loosely placed it on himself. He was standing with his hard cock pointing straight out when Donnie turned, and came back to him with the drinks, smiling.

Donnie held Max's drink to his mouth and turned it up for him until the last drop was gone. He took a sip of his own drink, before setting it on the table. Then he sat down so that his face was inches away from Max's hard cock. Looking up at him and barely concealing his delight, Donnie pulled Max's balls through the cock-ring and tightened it.

Max's head went back in erotic surrender when he felt the hot mouth engulf him, sucking; and then move underneath to engulf his trembling balls, giving them a hard, rough pull with his lips.

"Mmmmm," Max moaned. "It's yours, Big Daddy!—I'm yours...."

"You think it's that easy? You want me to fuck you… don't you?!" Donnie asked, menacingly, while looking up at Max's face, as he immediately went back to sucking, nibbling and biting Max's balls.

"Yessss," Max moaned. "Yesss, pleaseee… Big Daddy."

"You came here to be fucked, didn't you?" Donnie hissed.

"Yessss, Big Daddy? Mmmmmmm! Mmmmmmm! Mmmmm! What do you want me to say, Big Daddy?! I'll say anything… I'll do anything…. I couldn't stay away…."

"I want you to beg for it, ho! Beg me to fuck your ass! Beg for this dick!" He was sucking Max's balls, roughly, making sure Max was feeling his teeth.

Max felt his own legs going weak, and he crumbled to the couch.

"Pleassseee, Big Daddy… pleassseee! Pleassseee… fuck me… please… please fuck me, Big Daddy…." Max begged through bated breaths, consumed, out of his mind with desire.

Donnie placed Max on his knees on the couch. Oiling himself from one of the many oil-filled bottles he kept strategically placed about the Lodge, he squirted some onto Max. Then, he rammed his huge cock into Max's pleading, trembling, hot ass so hard, it knocked the breath out of him!

"Huummm! Aahhhhhhh! Oohhhhh!!" Max gasped as the thick, round head of Donnie loaded cock pierced and lodged itself inside!

Instantaneously, Donnie slapped Max's ass with his bare hand as hard as he could.

Max cried out again!

"Beg for it!" he demanded, enraged! "Beg for this dick, you mutha-fuckin' ass-ho, fuck! Don't stop begging me for it!"

"Give it to me, Big Daddy… whooaaa! Pleassseee… fuck me, Big Daddy! Whooaaa! Please… fuck me, Big Daddy!" he cried, with sweat and tears streaming down his cheeks.

Angry with himself for not being able to control his feelings for Max anymore, Donnie was slapping Max's ass between each thrust. Pushing his huge member deeper and deeper into the thick, hot tunnel that was being forced open to receive more and more and more.

"You thought you could walk away from this dick, bitch?! Yo'ass was made for this dick!" Donnie declared. "You love this dick, baby!—And... I own this hot... thick... tight-ass pussy!" Donnie rambled as he rammed his engorged member deeper and deeper into Max. "You know you love this dick, bitch! Don't you love it?!"

"Yessss, Big Daddy.... Whooaaa... I love it! It's yours, Big Daddy! I love it! Oohhhhhhhh... aahhhhhhhh.... It's yours, Big Daddy!" Max uttered through his moans. He was in that zone of ecstasy and pain, where he knew he would say anything to stay. He was in that zone where he could feel both his mind and body giving in to the force of nature he felt entering, dominating, consuming his entire being with each deliciously powerful, painful thrust.

"Huh... huh! Huh!! You love this dick, don't you, baby?!" Donnie demanded somewhat softer, breathing hard.

"Yeesss, Big Daddy, I love it...."

"Yeesss, you love this dick and you love me... mmmmm... for giving it to you like this, don't you, baby? Don't you?!"

"Yeesss, Big Daddy... yeessss...."

"Whooaaa, baby, my dick's all the way into this sweet ass! Mmmm! I own this ass, baby... you love it! Say it!" Donnie ordered, sending a hard slap to Max's right bun.

"I love it, Big Daddy.... It's yours, Big Daddy.... I love it.... Fuck! Take it, Big Daddy! Take it! Yeesss! Yeesss! Yeess!" Max heard himself crying in ecstatic surrender.

"Uuhhhhmmmm.... Good fuckin' ass, baby! Huhhh... huhhh! Is it good, baby?!"

"Ummm—huhhhhh, it's so good, Big Daddy! You hurt me soooo good! You fuck me soooo good, Big Daddy! You hurt me so good! Uuhhhhhhh.... Mmmmmm.... Give it to me, Big Daddy!"

On their knees, all 13 inches of Donnie's huge cock was buried in Max, now. He was leaning over his back, licking his words into his ear.

For Donnie, the control he felt over Max at that moment sent an ecstasy through his body that he had experienced too rarely. It was the ecstasy of sexual domination, and the fulfillment of being totally inside another person. Totally in control.

"Don't move! Don't... move!" he whispered, breathlessly, lying on Max's back with his huge cock planted in him to the hilt. "Damn baby, I can feel every move you make! Everything... in you.... Your ass feel soooo damn good! Soooo sweet...." Then, "Aahhhhhh... shit!! Let me fuck it! Uuhhh! Uuhhhh! Let me fuck it! Uuhhhhh! I'm cumming... Whooaaa! I'm cumming, baby! Aahhhhhhhhh," he moaned as he exploded.

Max felt the hot liquid filling him. The glorious, hot liquid spreading it's heat throughout his quivering body! It made him cry out, too.

"Aahhhhhhh, I love you, Big Daddy.... I love you.... Mmmmmm!" he cried.

Donnie rested on Max's back for a while after it was over, oblivious to Max's words.

Max lay motionless, still moaning his ecstasy. Donnie had not loosened the cock-ring, allowing him to cum. Max knew there was more to come.

As they lay there, they both knew that this time, this fucking, something had passed between them—an understanding. Donnie knew he owned Max. Max knew it too. Without saying it, they both knew that Max would never go home again.

Slowly, Donnie pulled out.

First, he refilled their drinks. Then, bringing him a robe and towel, he dried his cum from Max's ass, before turning him onto his back and staring at his face as he dried his engorged balls and cock. The cock-ring he was wearing was still tight. He was still hard.

Max lay there, hoping Donnie would relieve him with his mouth. He didn't. Instead, Donnie put back on his sweats, and left.

Disappointed, Max lay there not knowing what to expect, daring not to remove the cock-ring. His disappointment didn't last long. Because, no sooner had he finished the drink did he feel that old familiar sensation sweep over his body causing his conscious to quickly begin slipping away. But not before he felt the hot mouths consuming him.

Who?! Did the triplets come back? Donnie?!

He felt his cock being consumed by the fiery hot mouth as it pulled and sucked. He felt the hot, moistness as it consumed first one ball, then them both. He felt the wet hot tongue and fingers of the third one licking and massaging his anus, before he faded completely into a sweet, delicious nothingness.

Mmmmm... my nipples! Aahhhhh...

Chapter XIV

Max awakened a short time later in another place, on a bed face down with a slant-board beneath him. To his surprise, he realized his wrists were bound and tied down. It was very dark, and he knew it was late. The erotic sensations he had passed out feeling were still consuming him. And, along with his own moans and cries, they were awakening him.

"Uuhhhmmmm... whooaaa... ooaahhhhhh...." he sighed.

Coming around, he heard Donnie's voice. It was low and close to his ear, almost menacing.

"See how good I can make it for you, baby?!"

He tried to answer, but he could only moan longingly, as he felt his buns being pulled apart and the thick, rough tongue licking his ass, then pressing into it in a drilling fashion that made him feel certain it would enter!

"I've got three niggas getting your shit, baby... and... you can have this every day. You want it every day, baby?! You want me to let them suck your shit, every day?!"

"Yeesss, Big Daddy! Whoooaaaaahhhh!" Max cried, breathlessly. "I... want... you...."

"You can have it every day, baby... but, you've got to have it all! You've got to let me give all of it to you.... You've got to be *my* bitch... *my* ass-pussy ho.... You've got to want to be my ass-pussy ho, if you want to be sucked and fucked like this every day! You've got to love your Big Daddy... and let your Big Daddy love you! Do you want it, baby?! Do you?!" Donnie demanded, as the suckers ecstasy-laden tongues consumed Max in the dark.

"Aahhh—Oohhh... yeessss, I want it, Big Daddy.... I'm yours, Big Daddy!" he cried, panting breathlessly.

"But... do you love your Big Daddy?" Donnie demanded, pushing the one licking Max's anus away, and positioning himself there. "You gonna give your Big Daddy everything he wants?!"

"Yeesss, I love you, Big Daddy.... I love you.... I love you...."

The one sucking his cock was underneath the slant-board. The one sucking his balls was on his knees behind them. And Donnie was standing straddling them, his huge cock poised to enter Max's hot, moist, waiting tunnel. The one Donnie pushed aside was holding Max's cheeks apart. Donnie's massive member plummeted into Max's anus like a drill, thrusting himself halfway into Max before he stopped!

They were both moaning and breathing loudly.

"Mmmm-huh! Yeesss…. Can I make you my bitch, baby?! You want me to make you my ass-pussy-ho—bitch? Huh?! Tell me you want me to make you my ass-pussy ho!" Donnie demanded, rhythmically plunging himself in deeper, now.

"I want…. I want…."

"I own yo'ass, baby!" Donnie slapped Max's ass brutally hard. "You love how I do it to you… you love it!"

"Yesss, Big Daddy!," Max moaned.

"This is what I made you for! You know you love it! And you know you love me!" He slapped his ass again.

"Yesss, Big Daddy!" Max cried.

"Now, say you want me to make you my bitch! Say you want to be my ass-pussy ho!"

"I'm your ass-pussy ho, Big Daddy…." Max cried through bated breathes. "I want it, Big Daddy… I'm your ass-pussy bitch! Pleasseee, Big Daddy! I want it!"

"You'll never leave this dick, again, baby! Not after this! You'll never leave your Big Daddy, again!" Donnie declared. He was looking, fucking and talking as if he was in a trance—machine-like.

Again, his cock was buried in Max to the hilt. His chest was on Max's back, resting on his arms. "You ready for this, baby?! Huh?! You ready for ecstagony?!!"

He didn't wait for an answer.

With his huge cock buried in Max, he said to the others:

"Make him my bitch…. Give it to him!"

And with that, the two suckers now became tormentors! They simultaneously began biting the tender meat they had seconds ago been licking and sucking. They allowed their teeth to sink into him deep enough to cause excruciating pain, but not deep enough to break the skin!

It was the first time Max had ever felt such sharp, intense, penetrating pain, and agony, and such a helplessly erotic ecstasy—all at the same time. It caused his body to tremble violently out of control! His gyrations made him eagerly fuck Donnie's massive member planted deep within him. It was as if it had become a part of him. Rocking! Shaking!!

"Fuck Big Daddy, baby! Mmmm" Donnie moaned. "Aahhhhh! Fuck your Big Daddy!"

Max couldn't breathe. He couldn't speak. He couldn't control the way his body shook. Both tears and sweat poured from him. Panting, he could only feel the ecstasy of the pressure of Donnie's cock filling him—moving with him—and the agony of the teeth as they gripped ever mercilessly tighter onto his most tender meat.

Before he could say anything or even realize he could speak, Donnie ordered:

"Let up! Let up!"

Then, the biters suddenly became soothing lickers and suckers once again. Max stopped shaking and started breathing, moaning and sobbing uncontrollably.

"That's ecstagony, baby!" Donnie licked into his ear. "That's how I make you my ass-pussy bitch."

Then, "Give it to him!" he ordered, and the suckers instantly sent their teeth in once more, sending Max's body into the fucking trembles again!

This time Donnie let them bite Max's cock and balls even longer, savoring the trembling sensations his hugely engorged member was enjoying being buried in Max's gasping, shaking ass.

Finally, he ordered, "Let up!" only to give Max a chance to rest for an instant, and breathe. Then, "Give it to him! Eat his ass up! Bite those balls!" Donnie quickly ordered again. "Bite'em hard!! This is my bitch! This is mines, baby! This is how I fuck my shit! I own you.... You're my ass-pussy ho! My slave!" he rambled into Max's ear. "Your ass is gonna be aching before I'm through with it tonight, baby! You're gonna fuck your Big Daddy because your ass belongs to me!"

He let them bite Max even longer before he gave the order to let up this time.

"Pleasseee, Big Daddy!" Max cried, out of his head with the pain, and the pleasure, of it all. "I'll do anything you want.... I'll be whatever you want! I love you, Big Daddy! I love...."

"Then, beg for it, bitch!" Donnie shouted. "Beg for ecstagony!"

"Give it to me, Big Daddy," Max heard himself crying, lost in ecstagony! He was in total surrender to the shear ecstasy and agony of it—and to Donnie.

"Bite his ass!" Donnie ordered.

Hearing what he wanted to hear, he was on his knees now, pumping Max's trembling, shaking ass with a power and a fury that could only mean he would soon blow. "I love yo'ass too, baby! I love this ass-pussy!" he declared.

He slapped Max's ass, and gripped his cheeks pulling them apart. He pressed his flesh tightly against Max's trembling ass until it was hard to tell where one ended and the other began. "Get it off!! Get the cock-ring off!" he ordered, "I'm gonna... cum.... Aahhhhhh!!! Whooaaaaa!!!! I want you to cum, baby! Cum down that nigga's throat!" Donnie ordered slapping Max's trembling buns.

And that's the way he came. So deep inside Max, filling every inch of him, that he had to strain against the force of his own cum to keep from pushing himself out.

Max was cumming too, in an explosion itself so dynamic that it made his body continue convulsing, even when there was nothing left to come out.

"I'll be anything you want, Big Daddy!" he sobbed, as waves of ecstagony washed over him. "I'll be whatever you want."

He had never felt what he was feeling now. His cock, his balls and his entire being was throbbing and aching. But for Max, it was a most deliciously erotic ache. At that moment, he knew it was an ache he would crave, forever.

Exhausted, the slant-board removed, Donnie and the suckers lie where they were until they all settled down, and all was quiet.

Then Donnie ordered them away.

In the darkness, Max couldn't tell where they were or whether or not they had left the room. He could only feel Donnie's presence.

118

Donnie moved around on the bed so that he was lying in front of him. In the dark, he turned Max onto his side and began caressing his aching balls. His mouth was so close to his sore, limp cock that Max could feel him breathing on it.

Momentarily, he heard himself moaning quietly.

"Your dick's sore, ain't it, baby?!" Donnie whispered. "Your shit's aching?!" He was caressing and squeezing his balls.

"Yeesss, Big Daddy," Max gasped through his erotic agony, unable to soothe them with his still bound hands.

"Mmmmm... big balls...." Donnie whispered again, while squeezing Max. "I like hurting big, juicy balls, baby!" he said, "Can I put a hurtin' on these big, hot, juicy balls, baby?!"

A minute ago Max felt totally satisfied, but Donnie's words, squeezes and caresses were suddenly stirring the ache in him again.

"Yeesss, Big Daddy.... I'm yours.... Yeesss," he sobbed, knowing he would, and wanting to take the pain.

Now Donnie took Max's sore, limp cock into his hot, sucking mouth, simultaneously sending four of his fingers into him.

"Uummmmm," Donnie moaned and whispered, "I'm gonna crème you now, baby! That other nigga got your cum... but, I'm gonna get your crème!"

Max felt the fingers pressing and massaging a place at the base of him, pumping him. He felt the juices stir at his core! And, he purred like a cat as his juices swelled and flowed from him, like white-hot lava oozing from a volcano, down Donnie's hot, waiting throat.

Each pump sent a surge through Max that felt like pure nirvana. His mind and his body were totally gone. His ecstasy was complete, his cries were automatic.

"Ooooh—aahhhh! Godddd, Big Daddddddy! Take it! I'll do anything... anything you want! Whooaaaa! I'm your ass-pussy... ho, Big Daddddddy... I'm your ass-pussy ho! Pleaseee, Big Daddy.... It's sooo good! You hurt me soooo goooood...." he moaned.

Donnie had complete control over Max, now. Now, without taking his fingers out, he grabbed his sore, throbbing cock with his left hand squeezing it, holding it aloft, as he took his aching balls into his mouth. Donnie placed his thumb between Max's balls, keeping his fingers on the spot in him. Pinning Max's left

119

leg back with his own leg, Donnie sank his teeth into Max's balls and the base of his cock.

Again, Max's body went into an uncontrollable tremble. He was a quivering mass under the waves of this new ecstagony.

"Mmmmmm!" Donnie moaned. "I gonna swell'em up, tonight, baby! I'm gonna give you some big-ass balls tonight!"

Again his teeth sank into Max's most tender meat, and this time he shook his head like a hungry beast ripping a piece of meat from a kill, sending his captive's body into a trembling, quivering mass of ecstagony. Then, just when he felt Max could take no more, Donnie withdrew his teeth and began sucking and kissing and licking Max's bulging agony, but only for an instant as he took him in and out of ecstagony like that, over and over again—until that night was over.

* * * *

Alone, the next morning, Max rolled over onto his belly and awoke abruptly when he immediately felt pain between his legs. He rolled back over onto his back and moaned as he touched himself. Through the pain he could tell his balls were not only sore, but swollen to at least twice their normal size it seemed. Through the pain he continued to touch himself as he remembered everything about the day before Donnie. Laying there he knew he would never go back to the life he had known before. And with that knowledge, he continued touching himself, because he wanted to feel the pain. Suddenly, what was pain had turned into ecstagony as he lay there alone for as long as he could take it, touching and hurting himself.

Chapter XV

"Baby!" Donnie called, when Max entered the kitchen later that morning and found him there eating breakfast, alone. "Come here... let me look at you," he said, wiping is mouth with the back of his hand.

Max came to where he sat and stood there without saying a word, as Donnie untied the belt of his robe revealing his swollen nakedness. Even his breasts were swollen.

"You're beautiful, baby!" Donnie said, reaching up and squeezing a nipple. "If only these boobs were as big as these balls!" Donnie said, staring up at him. Max was looking straight ahead. Now Donnie's hand came down and cupped Max's balls, giving them a squeeze.

Max moaned and closed his eyes to the erotically-wicked pain Donnie's hand was causing.

"You hungry, baby? You haven't eaten since you came back. You want some breakfast?" His voice was soothing as he spoke, still looking up at Max, his hand still on Max's swollen balls.

"Yessss," Max sighed, breathlessly. He knew anything could happen. He felt weak.

"I think I want some nuts with my breakfast, baby. I want to eat some more nuts... and hear you scream in ecstagony. Like you did last night.... You see, I know how much you need the agony. You need to feel the pain, don't you?" he said and squeezed Max's balls hard.

"Whooaaahhh!" Max cried. "Yesss, Big Daddy...."

"Look at you!" Donnie said delightfully excitedly, looking at Max's already swollen cock as it became hard and began to swell, even more. "I believe you *do* want some more!"

Coming back up at Max's face, Donnie slipped his fingers into him once again. They knew precisely where to touch.

"Aahhhhhhh," Max sighed, standing there. He felt as if he would melt.

"Put your hands on my head..." Donnie ordered, "...guide it in."

Max obeyed.

Donnie took his cock into his mouth once more, and his fingers began to pump him.

Max's head went back and he closed his eyes tightly, sighing and moaning—and feeding himself to his master. As Donnie, once again, took command of him with several long, powerful shank-length sucks. Then, taking it out, Donnie said:

"You want some breakfast, and I want some more crème!" He was up now. He grabbed Max's wrist. "Get your ass over here," he ordered, leading him to the red leather divan, along a wall, that ended on one side underneath a large window. Donnie laid Max on it. Then, he pulled a tray across Max's chest and belly, and locked it into slots on the wall that appeared to be made specifically for that purpose, so that Max lay trapped underneath it.

"You're hungry? You want to eat?" Donnie asked excitedly, placing bread, fruit, cheese and sausage on the tray. "Eat breakfast, baby," he ordered, "while I get some more crème!" he said, sending his fingers back into Max's anus.

"Aahhhh...." Max moaned, unable to eat, barely able to control his hands gripping the tray, tightly.

"Eat!" Donnie ordered, just before his mouth grasped Max's cock.

Max was hungry and he tried to eat, but his breath was coming in short gasps, as Donnie's fingers worked in him and his sucks drew in whatever juices he had left. The erotic ecstasy he felt made trying to control his body useless. The only moves he could make were involuntary. He couldn't think. He could only feel and pant, sigh and moan, as Donnie took him.

"Is this mines... baby?" Donnie demanded between shank-long, hard sucks, and his fingers continued pumping. "Do I own yo'ass?!"

"Yeesss! God! Yeesss!" Max cried, erotically unaware of the tears running down the sides of his face.

Donnie's sucks were hard, and powerfully. Then, "Yes, what?!" he demanded.

"Yeesss, Big Daddy... I'll be whatever you want.... I'm yours, Big Daddy...."

"You're my ass-pussy ho... baby! Now... say it!" Donnie demanded.

"I'm—I'm your ass-pussy ho, Big Daddy.... I'm your ho!" Max cried, breathlessly.

"Keep saying it!" Donnie ordered. "I want you to know what you are!"

"Mmmm—Big Daddy! I'm… mmmmm—I'm your ass-pussy ho…." Max cried.

Keeping his fingers in him, he grasped his cock, placing the fingers of his left hand along the bottom, blocking off Max's semen flow, exposing his swollen balls. Donnie used his mouth, tongue and teeth in turn on his balls, first licking, then sucking, then biting them, once again sending Max's body into a trembling mass of convulsive ecstagony.

Looking at his right hand up close, Donnie drew his fingers together. And slowly, he sent his fist into Max's trembling anus, while sinking his teeth into the base of his cock and balls.

"Oohhhh… God!!! Aaahhhhh! Uummmm…" Max cried out in astonished, erotic agony. His ass arched up slightly, only to force Donnie's teeth deeper into his most tender meat. Then, he fell back to the divan, sending Donnie's hand deeper into him.

"Aahhh…. I'm your bitch! I'm… oohhhh! I'm yours, Big Daddy…. I'm…. Oohhhh… aahhhhh… uummmm…." he cried as Donnie sent his teeth and his fist deeper into him.

"You belong to me, baby!" he hissed, looking up at Max's face. "This belongs to me!" Again, his teeth went into Max's balls and his fist went in even deeper. "This is what your ass needs…. This is what it was made for! You need the agony… don't you?!"

"Yeessss, Big Daddy…. Yesss!" Max cried, as Donnie worked his ecstatic magic.

"Beg for it, baby! Beg me to bite your balls," Donnie ordered, sending his hand in a little deeper.

"Oohhhh… aahhhhh… bite me, Big Daddy!" he begged. "Bite me!"

And once again Donnie's teeth tore at Max's balls as if to rip them off.

Max's body fell into trembling convulsions.

"Keep begging for it, baby…. Keep begging me!" Donnie demanded. "Or, I'll bite'em off!!"

"Mmmm… please… bite me, Big Daddy…. Please!"

Donnie, enjoying how he felt inside, kept licking and sucking Max's cock and swollen balls and sending both his teeth and his fist into him deeper. He had gotten his fist in well pass his wrist, and was thoroughly enjoying the feel of it.

"I own you, baby... you're my bitch! My ass-pussy ho.... Now, say it!" he ordered, sitting up and rubbing Max's belly, keeping his hand and arm in him.

Max knew it was true.

Now, he knew it was true. He knew what he had become. He knew that somewhere in him all along he wanted it to come to this—and now here he was.

"I'm... your ass-pussy ho... Big Daddy.... Bite me, Big Daddy.... I'm yours...." he cried.

"Now, beg for ecstagony! That's what you want! You want... you need to feel this pain, don't you?! You want ecstagony!" Donnie was forcing his fist, commandingly.

"Yeesss, Big Daddy! I want it! I want ecstagony!" he sobbed, as his tears streamed down, and sweat poured from his body.

Looking with pleasure at the helpless, erotic torment of what was happening on Max's face, Donnie held his cock and balls aloft, then slowly he began guiding his fist in-and-out of him.

"I—I want the pain, Big Daddy!" Max sobbed openly, breathlessly. "I want the pain! I'm... yours, Big Daddy!" he cried.

The excitement of seeing Max in absolute surrender and hearing him beg made Donnie's own organ bulge to its limit.

He had won!

"Then, turn yo'ass over!" he ordered, slowly withdrawing his arm and fist.

When it was out, Max's body relaxed. Donnie unlatched the tray and pushed it away. Then he positioned Max on his knees on the divan, and leaned him across the center uplift with his ass toward the large window. On his knees behind him, Donnie rammed the huge head of his organ into him.

"This is what you came back for, ain't it?! This is what you crave!" he said while ramming it in deeper. "Ain't it?!" he demanded.

Sucking his breath in between his teeth, "Yessss, Big Daddy.... Goddd! Yessss!" Max cried.

"And... you've got it, baby! Now... beg! I want you to beg for it! I want to hear you scream for it!" he was thrusting his rock-hard cock in and out, and going in deeper each time it entered.

"G-o-d! Give it to me, Big Daddy... pleaseeee.... Fuck! Fuck me! I want it.... Aahhhhh... pleaseeee, Big Daddy!" Max pled loudly, breathless, sweating, crying and moaning as Donnie's punishingly-hot, hard rod plunged into him again and again.

Did he want it to be over? Did he want it to end? His whole body was aching and extremely sore by now. But as deep down within him as was Donnie's pounding rod, he knew he didn't want it to ever end.

"Uuhhhhh... your ass is so damn good, baby! My dick loves this ass-pussy! You're my ass-pussy ho, baby!" Donnie cried. "Your ass is soooo damn good!" he moaned, throwing himself over Max's back, wrapping his arms around him, and cumming deep inside.

Max still lay on the divan, naked and too sore and exhausted to move, when the triplets entered. Donnie was tying the rope on his sweatpants.

"Doctor... ah—somebody called... said he's on his way," one of them said to Donnie.

"Take him upstairs, and clean him up. And, get the hair off his ass before Doc gets here," Donnie ordered. They were towel drying the sweat from Max's drenched body.

"Oh! And feed him," Donnie ordered. "He didn't get full... of food.... And boys, keep him feeling good.... Later, we're going to my cabin."

Immediately, two of them hoisted Max up so that his arms were over their shoulders, and then they carried him out.

Donnie knew he had been brutal. As he straightened up the kitchen, he told himself: *Max deserves it... he wants it that way. Besides, I was mad as hell!*

Drying his arms and hands, he sat back down to finish his breakfast.

He knows he wants it! He came back for it?

He felt good. He felt satisfied knowing Max belonged to him. As he sat back down to eat, he couldn't remember the last time he felt so good just knowing he would have Max that way, and any other way, whenever he wanted. Sitting there, finishing his breakfast, he knew he would do it to him just as brutally, *if that's what it takes to keep him*, he thought.

As he sat there, totally satisfied with himself, Pretty Boy strolled in pass him, looking at him, knowingly. He grabbed the robe Max had been wearing.

"Uh-huh, wringing wet! Last night wasn't enough," Pretty Boy said, taking a seat at the table a few places away from Donnie.

Donnie didn't reply.

So, Pretty Boy broke a few grapes off from the bunch on the table and popped a couple into his mouth before he continued.

"Now we're taking him to the cabin." He ate another one.

Still, Donnie said nothing.

"All I got to say is… you may be fucking his ass off, baby. But he sure the hell's fucking with your head."

Donnie was feeling too mellow to let Pretty Boy's words perturb him.

"Fuck you," he said, simply.

"Nah-un!" Pretty Boy pulled on the word, pushing his chair back from the table and getting up. "You're not putting that thang in this!" He stood and slapped his ass. Then strolled toward the door.

"Don't want to," Donnie said, smiling even broader. "I got what I want."

Pretty Boy was just able to close the door behind himself in time to keep Donnie from seeing how his last words had cut him to the bone. Silently, he fell back against the door, and clutching his arm and the wet robe around his stomach, he stuffed his knuckles in his mouth to keep from crying out! He felt faint. It was the first time he realized how deeply Donnie felt about Max.

He had never been jealous of Sharon or anyone else Donnie had ever been with, because he had always been Donnie's number one man, and confidante. He knew how to satisfy him orally, so even without the physical sex act between them since that first time, he had always believed that Donnie loved him, and wanted him. Now he realized that might not be so.

But—I love you!—You gotta love me! You've always loved me. That's why you keep me here.

His head was spinning!

I'll do whatever you want! I'd fuck you—if you want...me! You—I love you! Why can't you see that?!

"Is he in there?"

So engrossed in his thoughts, Pretty Boy heard Dr. Stewart's voice before he even realized he was standing before him.

"Are... you all right?" the doctor asked, looking at Pretty Boy, curiously.

"Yeah... sure," Pretty Boy said, straightening himself up. "I must have ate something.... It's just so much shit going on around here! I just have to get my head on straight... that's all."

"Is he here?" Dr. Stewart asked again.

"Be my guest... he's waiting for you," Pretty Boy said, stepping away from the door. He threw Max's wet robe over his shoulder, and managed to sashay off down the hall in his usual airy manner.

Chapter XVI

The cabin in the mountains was set in seclusion on twelve acres. If you didn't know the private drive was there, you would miss it. Trees obscured the front of the property, and their canopies formed a tunnel down the long, gravel drive.

The cabin looked like a stylish Tudor home when you came to it. In the back a well-manicured lawn that looked to be the length and width of a football field, stretched out beyond the house to the woods and the stream. In the back, the cabin looked very much like an ancient Egyptian palace with a Jacuzzi on an exquisite and elaborately furnished veranda, as well as a swimming pool. It was a breathtakingly beautiful place.

As the sun shined down on Donnie Soledad Williams, clad only in pajama bottoms, sitting at a table next to the wading pool in deep thought, there was no solace to be found on his handsome, brooding brow. He was staring out toward the trees and drinking a cup of coffee when he heard Max stirring within.

Why did I bring him here? He wondered, *why did I send Pretty Boy and the triplets back? Why did I let his ass get under my mutha-fuckin'skin?!*

There had been a few others who had been able to endure his mighty cock, and they had been good. But now he was wondering, *Why is it different with Max?* Feeling his cock stir, he wondered, *why do I want this mutha-fucka so god-damn much?!*

He finished the coffee, placing the cup on the table, and went inside.

He found Max in the bathroom, peeing. Thoughts of that first time he had taken him suddenly flashed through his head. Neither said anything to the other until Max finished.

"How does it feel?" Donnie asked, concerned.

"I think you know," Max said quietly, closing his robe and slowly coming toward Donnie who stood at the doorway. He moved aside to let Max pass.

"I mean, how do *you* feel?"

"Sore... tired," Max replied, and fell back onto the pillows on the bed.

"That's how you're going to feel, if we're going to do this... if you're kicking it with me, baby," Donnie said, without moving from where he stood. "I told you last night, and I'm telling you now. There's nobody here but you and me. If you don't want this… if you don't want to be with me… here… I'll get you a ride. Hell! I'll take you—you can walk right out that fucking door."

Max sat up as if to respond. But he didn't say anything.

Instead, he dropped his head and let the pain that Donnie had bestowed upon him radiate throughout his entire body. With his eyes closed, he brought both hands up to his neck and shoulders and threw his head back, massaging himself. A sigh escaped his throat as he did this, and Donnie saw him move underneath the robe.

Now Donnie came to the bed and sat beside him.

Taking Max's hands down, Donnie turned him and slowly began massaging his neck and shoulders.

"You were *made* for me, baby," he whispered in Max's ear. "They worked your ass… and stretched it… and then… they presented your ass to me on a silver platter!"

Max kept his eyes closed as Donnie massaged him. Listening.

"And your ass felt soooo god-damn good… I wanted it! I paid for it!" Donnie continued talking as though he was explaining this to himself. "Hell! I'm still paying for it!"

When Max heard Donnie say that, it was the first time he had thought about money since he came back. For, he had already realized he hadn't come back for the money.

"You know you wanted me to hurt you! You wanted… no, you needed ecstagony! God! My dick do love giving it to this sweet ass!" Closer to Max's ear now, he continued: "And… I'm gonna keep on paying for it! I'm gonna keep on giving it to you, baby…. Yeah!" Donnie's growing excitement was evident in his voice—his breathing. "Because my dick do love fucking this tight, hot ass here! I love fuckin'it!"

Now except for their heavy breathing, neither said anything. Deliberately, slowly, Donnie lay Max down on his stomach, and straddled him. Leaning forward, stretching out Max's arms, only their breathing gave away their feelings. Straightening back up, Donnie rested his slowly engorging member on Max's ass and continued massaging him before he started talking again.

"Ecstagony! That's the only way you can take it… You fight it so hard, baby, because you don't wanna accept how much you love the dick… how much you love taking it with the pain!"

As sure as Max knew anything, he knew that what Donnie was saying was true. Hearing and accepting the truth—and feeling Donnie's hands on him—made him feel as if he was becoming a part of Donnie. Suddenly he felt soft, melting, as he was becoming part of Donnie's hands. He knew he would be whatever Donnie wanted him to be.

Max's breathes came in gasps as Donnie continued.

"I know why you need ecstagony, baby…. Uh-huh!" Donnie chuckled, as he parted Max's buns and sent the oil-filled syringe into him. "Hell… I know why I need it…. Why I have to give it to this sweet, black ass," he said so longingly you would have thought he was a starving man describing a delicious meal. "Why I need to hurt you, baby…. Why I need ecstagony! On your knees!" he ordered. And as soon as Max complied, Donnie sent his left arm around Max's hips, pinning his captive, and grasping his balls and dick at the base. Then, Donnie's fist slowly, meticulously disappeared into the oil-oozing, burnt-bronze opening!

"Aaaahhhhhhhh!" Max sighed, long and hard.

"Mmmmm…. Yeah! …. I have to hurt you, baby," Donnie said ecstatically, sending his fist in further. He began fist-fucking Max, pumping him.

"Oohhh! Aaaahhhhhhh!" Max cried.

"Just like you have to let me… hurt you." Donnie said, as his arm went in deeper still.

Max could no longer hold himself up on his knees.

Slowly, Donnie guided Max down to the bed, keeping his fist planted firmly in him. Donnie's shoulder and chest lay across Max's butt. His left hand was underneath Max, clutching his balls. Donnie used his legs to hold Max's left leg and thigh out of the way, as his right fist and arm began the rhythmic pumping in-and-out of Max's anus.

"Oohhh! Oohhh! Aahhh! Aahhh!" Max gasped with each pump, as a terribly terrific, trembling, erotic pain now consumed him. Now, unbound, with just the two of them, he gave himself over to it, totally.

This was between him and Donnie only, now.

Absolute abandonment!

"Yo'ass feels so damn good, baby! No matter how I'm fuckin' you… yo' ass feels so fuckin' good to me!" Donnie declared.

Laying so that he could clearly see how much Max was taking, he twisted his arm as he sent his fist into Max this time.

"You see, I have to hurt it, baby…. 'Cause this belong to me!"

"Oohhh yeesss, Big Daddy!" Max cried. "Yeesss! Yeesss!"

"You know, I can do whatever I want to you?!"

"Yeesss!"

"I could rip you apart! Do you know that?! Huh?! I could rip you apart just as well as I can fuck yo'ass like this!"

"Yeesss! Oh God! You hurt me sooo… good! It's ripping me apart, Big Daddy! Yeesss! You hurt me so good!" Max exclaimed in a total erotic anguish—total ecstagony.

"But I can't destroy this ass… baby" Donnie said in a whisper, licking and kissing Max's buns, and resting his face on them so he could get the ultimate view of his fist and arm going in and out

Max's ass trembled with each impact! His cries, sighs and moans pierced the otherwise quiet, morning air, again and again.

And, Donnie took Max that way all morning long.

Chapter XVII

So, without words or a handshake, their *back end* agreement was made. Max would stay at Donnie's cabin, and Donnie would come practically every day. It didn't take long before a comfortable pattern was developing between them. Max could concentrate on his writing. He knew he belonged to Donnie exclusively, and Donnie took care of him.

There was an older couple who lived in a small house on the premises, though they were rarely in his cabin when Donnie was there, unless he wanted then to be there. They took care of the grounds, meals and cleaning.

All Max had to do was write, and keep himself ready for Donnie. He found neither one of these hard to do. Because, for the first time in his life, Max felt more contentment with what was happening in his life. Accepting things as they were, he actually flourished. The black twists in his hair hung almost two inches, thanks to the stylists Donnie sent to the cabin to do his hair. Looking very much like figures seen in the painting of ancient Egyptian workers from the Egyptian mural Donnie had on one wall in their bedroom, his body had become leaner and softer. Since he began taking the hormones Donnie had the doctor prescribe for him while he lay mending after their last fight, his breasts had grown to well over an A cup. Though his penis no longer reached the stiff, 7 inch erection it used to.

Max had noticed these particular changes, but now it didn't bother him. He had made the choice to change that day, sitting in his bathtub with the razorblade to his wrists. He knew what he wanted—needed. Now he had accepted it. He knew what he was. Max was amazed at the difference a couple of months could make in his mind, and in his body. For the first time in his life he was in love with what he felt was his true self, and with Donnie. And he was writing what he knew was the best stuff he had ever written.

Donnie kept his end of the agreement too. He took care that Max had everything he needed. He took care that Brian had everything he needed. He lied and told Kimberly that Max and the *woman* Brian said he saw him with had run off, probably together. To Donnie it only seemed like a half lie. Anyway, she believed him.

For the first time in a long time, with Max, Donnie was totally satisfied in his love life. He would leave the bar around five every morning, heading to the cabin—and Max.

* * * * *

"You feel sooo good!" Donnie whispered these words most mornings when he crawled in bed beside—or behind—the sleeping Max. Sending one arm over him, fumbling for the burgeoning nipples, soon they had grown ample enough so that when he was sleeping on his side, Donnie could bring them together in one hand. Then, he would pull and squeeze them until Max stirred and his breathing became loud with his arousal. The other hand Donnie would send underneath his waist, grasping his balls and cock. "Mmmmm…. You feel soooo fuckin' good!" Donnie would lick into Max's ear.

"Don-nie… you hurt it soooo fuckin' good," Max would reply.

By now Max was usually as fully awake as the drugs Donnie kept him supplied with would allow. His body reacted automatically, as soon as Donnie touched it. He had quickly grown accustomed to preparing himself for Donnie, and, sleeping naked.

"Turn over, baby!" Donnie whispered as soon as he heard Max's heavy, rhythmic breathing. "Turn over on your back."

Keeping his hand at Max's breasts, Donnie shifted his weight onto his arm and elbow to give Max room to turn. And then, he was at his lips as if to kiss or bite, but doing neither, deliberately edging up and away, escaping Max's groping mouth.

"Put your arms up over your head! You know what I'm gonna do! Don't you?" Donnie whispered, as Max obeyed. "Don't you?!" he insisted. When Max's answer didn't come soon enough: "Answer me!"

"Yeesss…" Max moaned. "They're so sore…."

Donnie was binding his wrists, tying them with a long scarf they kept anchored to the bed for that purpose.

"What am I gonna do?" Donnie pressed, again deliberately escaping Max's hot, groping mouth. He went back to the work of binding him. "Say it!" he ordered.

Max's chest was heaving as he whispered, "Bite… bite me!" Remembering the wicked exquisiteness of this ecstatic, new pain he was fast growing accustomed to—even desiring, he closed his eyes.

Donnie was at his tits, holding them just so the nipples were close enough for him to take them both into his mouth.

"Keep saying it!" he ordered, and Max's nipples disappeared into his hot, sucking mouth.

"Bite me," Max sighed, throwing his head back and arching to brace his body in anticipation of Donnie's teeth. Feeling only his hot tongue and the powerful pulls of his sucks, his body surrendered, melting. "Bite me!" he cried.

"You want'em sore," Donnie whispered between licks and sucks. "You like it when they're raw.... Don't you?!"

"Yesss...."

"Now, say it!"

"Bite me!" Max's answer was now sounding more like a plea, as he lay bound, feeling the ecstasy of Donnie's mouth on him.

"This is where it's at with yo'ass, baby! Right here!" He was lying on top Max, facing him. Resting on his elbows, his hands were grasping Max's breasts, holding the nipples together. He nibbled at them with his lips, capturing them, and running his hot tongue across the tops. "Right here... in these, big... beautiful... tiddies, baby!"

"Mmmmm.... Bite me, Big Daddy! Bite me... bite m...." Closing his eyes as tight as he could squeeze them, Max saw stars as Donnie's teeth clamped down on his nipples at the base. He could say nothing. His whole body stiffened as the fire from Donnie's teeth shot down into it. Bound, audibly gasping for air, all he could do was submit and surrender until Donnie stopped biting. Then Max drew in a deep breath. "Oohhh God! Oohhh God!" he cried. "You hurt me sooo good...."

Max's chest heaved as once again Donnie sank his teeth into him over and over again, deep enough to cause the agonizingly erotic painful ecstasy, but never deep enough to break the skin. But, Donnie would bite, suck and lick Max's nipples until he could taste their rawness. Finding his body being egged on by Max's submissive moans, cries and pleas, it was not until he made Max beg to be fucked did Donnie, in all his full glory, on his knees between Max's thighs, place first his left, then his right leg over his shoulders, and gave it to Max missionary style.

"Open your eyes!" he would order. Because he loved seeing Max's eyes flutter and almost close, uncontrollably, at his initial thrusts.

He was taking Max the way he knew Max loved most. He knew he had won. He knew he owned Max now, and he knew that for the first time with a man he was feeling something more than mere lust.   Just as he had done to get him, now Donnie Soledad Williams knew he would do whatever it took to keep him.

* * * * *

Max spent all his waking hours with Donnie, thinking about Donnie, getting ready for Donnie, and writing.   Writing, his poems had always been the way he could express his feelings.   Once, when he was younger, he thought he might one day become a poet, until someone told him all poets were sissies—and poor. Though no longer wanting to become a poet, he had never been able to stop writing poetry.   And though it had been months since he had written anything or even thought about writing, the writing came easy.

The first poem he wrote was:

A New Way to Love

How did you enter me so sweetly
Filling me completely

Giving me a new way to love

Telling me it's all right
Filling my head with delight
Consuming my days and night

With this new way to love

Should I have never known you
Would I have been inclined to

Know a new way to love?

Perhaps yes
Maybe no
But the one thing I do know

I love this new way to love.

His second poem:

You Make Me Cry with Pleasure

135

You make me cry with pleasure

Your mouth
  as hot as it is

Your hands
  as warm as they are

You
  as full as sure as real as you are

Find me
  waiting in the dark

Wanting
Hoping
Needing

You
  make me cry with pleasure.

Many mornings Mrs. Jeffries would prepare breakfast for the two of them, and always make her exit just before, or as Donnie was coming in. Max would rise early to eat with him. Then they would spend the morning together making love. In the afternoons while Donnie was sleeping, Max would sit nearby thinking and writing. And, as Max wrote, he would often feel within his bones that in times to come he would often think back on these times, and remember just how close to heaven he felt.

Chapter XVIII

Max loved walking around the premises finding new places to write, and thinking of new ways and places he and Donnie would make love—on a floater in the pool, in the evening in a hammock on the eastside of the cabin (the Jeffries were on the west), in the Jacuzzi, on the bathroom floor. They made love and he experienced ecstagony in every one of those places. But he saved his most precious place, a small cove at the edge of a brook that ran along the back of the property line, for the day he would present his book of poems to Donnie.

That day he asked Mrs. Jeffries to bring him 4 dozen red roses, and champagne.

Donnie was on his way.

Starting at the bedroom doors that lead out onto the patio, Max dropped rose petals, he had seen something like that in a movie, as he strolled across the large, groomed lawn to his cove. It was warm so we wore his short, black satin robe. He carried a fresh blanket under his arm, and the champagne in a basket with cheese and crackers, grapes, cherries, berries, and his manuscript of poems.

"Max? Are you in there?" Donnie called, dodging the low foliage canopy as he got close.

"Come in and see," Max replied, pouring the champagne.

Donnie peeped in to find Max seated on the blanket with the food spread out before him.

"I've got something for you," Max said, lifting a glass of champagne to Donnie.

"What the hell are you gonna think of next?!" Donnie asked, laughingly joining him. Taking the champagne, he lifted Max's hair out of the way and kissed him on the neck.

Max took his arm, stopping him before he could take a drink.

"A celebration toast," he said, "I've finished the book."

He held his drink in his right hand, and gave Donnie the manuscript with his left so that he could read the title, *A Book of Poems for Soledad.*

After reading the title, Donnie looked at Max, pleased. Then, they clinked their glasses and took their first sips of champagne.

"I have something else for you," Max said, taking the manuscript as Donnie removed his jacket, settling in. "It's the last poem."

Flipping to the last page, Max read:

"For Donnie

You come unto me
In the night

Like a cool blade
Entering
Awakening
A desire so deep
My body quakes
And sighs and
Surrenders
I have made it
Ready
For you
Mmmm.... Mmmmm!
I breathe
I am alive!
For you are
My light
My love
My life."

"It's beautiful...." Donnie said, smiling. "You saying you love your Big Daddy, baby?" he asked a bit too casually for Max's mood, as he lay back rubbing Max's ass through the black satin robe.

Max thought about the question for a few seconds, only, before he said: "Yeah."

It was one of those silent moments when they both knew that what had been said was true.

"Well," Donnie started, "I love yo'ass, too."

Pulling Max down to him, they kissed and Donnie slipped his hand inside Max's robe.

"Not yet, Big Daddy!" Max exclaimed, and pulled away. "I'm not through," he added.

Max moved between Donnie's legs. Donnie lifted himself to let Max pull his pants off.

Max was always amazed at the beauty of Donnie's chiseled physique. Everything was magnificently proportioned, except for the 13" phallus that had already reached its full potential. But on Donnie it looked absolutely right.

Rubbing his thighs, looking at him lying there in his full glory instantly took Max back to that Sunday afternoon when he first caught a glimpse of Donnie in the bathroom at his gym. Now he could admit to himself that somehow he knew, even then, that someday this day would come.

Donnie loved the way Max looked at him, now. He lay there with his hands behind his shaved head, with what could only be described as a satisfied smile on his face, watching Max looking at him.

Taking the bottle of champagne, Max lifted Donnie's head while holding the bottle to his lips, and he licked and kissed Donnie's mouth when the champagne spilled out. Taking Max's licks and kisses, Donnie's smile grew broader when Max poured champagne onto his neck, and licked and sucked it off. Donnie was softly sighing and stroking Max's back underneath the black satin robe, as Max poured more champagne onto his chest, and licked and sucked it up, too. Finally, Max poured champagne all around the huge cock, and kissed and licked and sucked until Donnie could take no more. He lifted his cock at the base, giving it to Max. And Max filled his mouth with champagne. Then he sucked in the huge head, and as much of the shaft as he could take.

"Aaahhhh…." Donnie sighed, feeling the coolness of the champagne and the warmness of Max's lips.

Max swallowed.

"Love… that… dick…." Donnie moaned.

Max sucked the huge phallus, amazed at how good and smooth it felt in his stretched open mouth, wishing he could take in more. Finally, coming up off the head and going down and around the sides to Donnie's balls, he licked, kissed and sucked them too. Then he turned Donnie over and poured champagne onto Donnie's ass, and his tongue followed the liquid down between the split to the puckered, silkiness of his ass. There it lingered long, hot, and deeply sweet.

"Aaahhhh!... suck it, baby! Suck it!" Then, finally:

"Turn yo'ass around!" Donnie ordered, breathlessly. And as Max complied, he was up on his knees behind him, fingering his ass to make sure he had gotten himself ready. He had. Donnie lubed his steaming rod, and leaning over him, grasping the back of Max's neck with his left hand, throwing his head back and closing his eyes, he used his right hand to guide himself in.

"Aahhhh!" Max moaned.

"You know why I love fucking your ass?" Donnie asked through clenched teeth. He was pumping Max doggy-style, on his knees leisurely, erotically. "Because each time my dick slices into your ass, it's like it's slicing into a little piece of heaven... baby!"

"Uummm!" Max moaned each time Donnie sank into him.

"Your tight... sweet... hot ass... baby! Taking all this dick," Donnie continued, sending himself all the way into Max, and holding it.

"Uummm! Uummm! Uummm!"

"And then, baby... when I pull out... it... just... closes back up... so tight." Only the massive head of his huge cock remained in Max. "I slice into it... again... like... this...." He was all the way into him, again. "And... I can feel... every tight-ass... muscle... in you! Damn, baby... it's sweet! Sooo good! Thick! Hot! Tight! Fuck!"

The rhythm of his thrusts had picked up, now, and so had Max's cries and moans.

"I had to get this, baby! I had to make it mine! After my dick tasted it that first time at the Lodge... I had to own it! You know that... don't you, baby?!"

"Yeessss, Big Daddy!" Max cried.

"And you love this dick... don't you, baby?"

"Yeesss, Big Daddy!"

"I knew you loved it... when I first fucked this sweet ass! Mmmmm! It feels sooo good," Donnie cried. "I knew you loved this dick!" Donnie plunged in. "Uummmmm! You feel that! You feel that, baby!"

"Mmmmmm... yeesss! Yes, Big Daddy!"

"You feel how good that feels?!" Donnie asked, holding himself deep within Max.

"God, yes! Yes!" Max cried.

"And… you love it! You love this dick… don't you?!"

"Aahhhh! Mmmmm! Yeesss… yeessss, Big Daddy…."

"Feel that!" Donnie said. "Whoooaaaa, baby! Feel that?!" he asked.

"Oohhh yesss, Big Daddy! Yes!"

"Then… tell me, baby! Tell me how good it feels!" he ordered, sticking it to him.

"It feels soooo good, Big Daddy!" Max cried. "It feels so good! Oohhhh… it feels so good!"

"Yeah!" Donnie hissed. "Keep it up!" he demanded, sensing the mounting pressure within himself.

"Fuck me, Big Daddy! Mmmmm!" Max's voice trembled. "You fuck me soooo gooood…. Mmmmm! You fuck me so good, Big Daddy…." Max cried. He wanted to stay there, right there, on the edge, in the zone with Donnie, forever.

Chapter XIX

For the first time in his life, Max felt like he was in love. He was happy being there for Donnie, and writing. When he came back to Donnie, he walked away from a life that still held only one regret for him—his son.

He wrote:

Looking for myself
I found you.

I love you
And in loving you
I nourished myself, cared for myself
And in loving you
I lost what was me—to you

Looking for myself
I learned
I am not you

I love you—but
I had to keep on
Looking for myself

And in looking for myself
I think I always knew
I had to lose you
when
I found myself.

* * * * *

One afternoon Donnie lay on the bed naked, talking about the boys' team going on a trip to Florida. Max, in an untied robe, stood staring out the glass doors past the veranda toward his favorite writing spot, listening to Donnie talking about his most recent visit with their sons at Hargrove's.

"I want to see my son," he said, suddenly, longingly.

"Your son wants to see you too, baby," Donnie replied.

Hearing this, Max turned and came to him. Donnie could see the hope and happiness on his face. He looked into Donnie's eyes, searchingly.

"Really?!" he asked, cautiously.

"Really," Donnie smiled. He felt good knowing he could let Max know he had been working to repair his relationship with Brian. It assuaged his guilt at having been the one who caused the rift in the first place.

Max smiled broadly.

"What did he say?!" he asked.

"Last week he asked if I could find you and ask you to come to the tournament next month. It's gonna be in Orlando. I've already reserved rooms for us...."

"Why didn't you tell me?!" Max asked, excited.

"I am telling you," Donnie replied. "I wanted to wait until I got everything set up—a room for you and Brian, one for me and Trey, and one for you and me!"

"He wants me to come? He told you to ask me? Why?!"

"Because I've been telling him how much you care about him. How much you miss him. That he's got a great dad... I must have finally gotten through to him... and, he really does misses you, man," Donnie said, sincerely.

"Is this for real?! I mean... Donnie?!"

"It's for real, baby. Coach is gonna bring the boys, and we'll fly down.... I've got the rooms, tickets, everything all set," Donnie said, and took a finger and placed a strand of Max's loose hair behind his ear.

"Donnie," Max said, and turned his head welcoming Donnie's finger into his mouth.

Sensuously he sucked it while staring longingly at Donnie's pleased face through liquid eyes filled with tears of happiness, desire and love.

"I love you," Max whispered, as he took Donnie's hand into his hands, and parting each fingers, he took each one in turn into his mouth. "I love you so much," he cried.

Slowly Donnie's hands clasped the sides of his face bringing him closer. First, he lightly touched his lips to Max's hungry mouth, then pressing harder, and harder still, as their tongues danced and played passionately with each other—a preamble to the dance that soon followed.

* * * *

"What's he doing here?!" Max asked, angrily, surprised at seeing Pretty Boy enter behind Donnie as they came into the bedroom.

It was a couple of weeks later.

Max hadn't seen Pretty Boy since his son saw them in his room on the bed together. Since coming back to Donnie, he placed all the blame on Pretty Boy for the rift between him and Brian.

The anger in Max's voice made Pretty Boy arrogantly swish into the room now, and slither up to Max who, wearing only a short robe, had stopped in his tracks.

"I'm here to show you how to hide those," Pretty Boy said, reaching toward Max's breasts.

Max knocked his hand away. "You're not going to touch me, you mutha-fuckin'bitch!" he said.

"It takes one to know one!" Pretty Boy retorted.

"Come on, Max," Donnie chimed in. "You've got to learn how to bind'em up, baby. You know, we can't have the boys seeing'em," he said.

Coming to Max. He lifted his chin to give him a peck on the lips. "Even though I love looking at 'em," he added, sending his hand inside Max's robe.

"I don't need him to show me a god-dam thing!" Max said, turning away. "Get him out of here, Donnie."

"I don't need this shit from your ass-pussy ho!" Pretty Boy said.

And, instantly, Max' turned and landed a right to Pretty Boy's jaw, sending him to the floor!

"Max!!!" Donnie said, surprised.

He was trying to help Pretty Boy up. But Pretty Boy snatched away from him and got up by himself. Trying to get to Max, Donnie held him off, preventing the fight.

144

"Give me the mutha-fuckin' keys, Donnie! I don't need this shit!" Pretty Boy insisted, while fumbling to remove an elastic contraption that looked like a back brace with holes cut out on the sides for arms and Velcro fasteners in back from the bag he carried, and threw it at Donnie—tears swelling in his eyes. "Give me the fuckin' keys!" he demanded.

Surprised and somewhat amused, Donnie tossed him the keys.

"Call and let me know when to pick you up," Pretty Boy said, haughtily, as he straightened himself up and closed his bag. He took one last look at Max. And, Donnie couldn't tell whether it was a look of hatred, envy or lust.

Then, he left.

Donnie tossed the breast-binding brace to Max, who caught it and examined it.

Sitting on the bed, Donnie kicked off his shoes.

"Now, what was that all about?" he asked. "I thought you liked Pretty Boy."

"Not just now," Max said. "He's the real reason Brian hates me."

"Brian don't hate you…. But, what are you talking about—*he's the reason*?" Donnie asked, innocently.

"I thought you did it, but now I know it was Pretty Boy's ass who set me up and let Brian see him sucking my cock all along!" Max explained.

"Damn! So, that's what happened that day?! No wonder the kid was so upset!" Donnie feigned.

"He must have looked like a woman to Brian," Max continued.

He had removed the robe and was trying to put on the brace, attempting to connect the Velcro fasteners along the back. Naked now, he moved to Donnie for help.

"At least, that's what he told Kimberly."

"Oh! That's why Kimberly kept asking me about your 'bitch'." Donnie chuckled as he clasped and pressed the last fastener, and patted Max's ass sending him off to view himself in the mirror. "You know, now that I think about it, when she described *her* it was a pretty good description of Pretty Boy! You know…. Your son saved your ass, baby," Donnie called to Max.

In the bathroom, Max pulled on some sweats. "This thing is as tight as hell! What do you think?" he asked, returning to where Donnie sat, while wiggling his upper body trying to loosen the brace.

"It'll do. You'd never know. Besides, you'll only have to wear it when we're with the boys," Donnie said, stretching out.

"I can't go swimming.. I can't sleep in it," he said, still wiggling.

He sat on the bed beside Donnie, who sent his hand underneath Max's top.

"We not going to go swimming," he said, loosening the brace. We've got an extra room, remember? Baby, you ain't gonna be wearing it when *we* go to bed."

* * * * *

Brian ran to his father after he got off the hotel bus in front of the hotel lobby.

"Dad!" he called, dropping his duffle bag.

"I missed you, son," Max said, embracing him, almost in tears.

"Dad!" Brian exclaimed, "I missed you so much!"

"Didn't I say when you let me know you were ready, I'd find him and bring him here?" Donnie asked, coming up to them with his son.

Trey extended his hand to Max.

"How are you, Mr. Newman?"

"Great! Thanks, man," Max replied, playing along. "Good to see you, Trey. Good to see you.. and Brian."

"Thanks, Mr. Williams," Brian said, almost simultaneously.

Now Donnie and Trey were off.

"If nothing's up, you guys want to hook up for dinner, later?" Donnie asked, leaving. "Give us a call." Donnie made the telephone sign with his hand to his ear.

Max watched as his arm came down and rested on his son's shoulders.

Somehow Max hoped Brian would have forgotten about what he saw that day at Donnie's. He had spent the last five months so much into his own gratification that he could at times, block out the past, including thoughts of his son. But whenever Donnie came to the cabin talking about Hargrove's and the boys, he was finding that harder and harder to do. He was never really in love with Kimberly, and he found it surprisingly easy to forget her. His son, though, was another matter.

Max noticed Brian seemed to grow more morose, adverting his eyes and talking less as the evening wore on. By the time they got back to their room, Max knew the memory of what Brian had seen had not gone away.

The conversation Max and his son had to have came that night, after dinner.

Brian came into the room and threw himself on his bed. He thumbed through a couple of sports magazines, while Max stood on the balcony gazing at the ocean, trying to think of a way to start the conversation.

I'll tell him the truth, he thought. *I'll just say, we need to talk. I'll say, you can ask me anything you want, and I'll tell you the truth.*

He stood there a minute longer, remembering how easy talking to his son use to be. He turned and stepped back into the room.

"Dad?" Brian said as soon as he came in.

"Yeah, son," Max replied, not knowing what his boy was about to say.

"Are you gay?" Brian simply asked.

The question stunned him! He was speechless.

Seeing the look on his father's face, now Brian stammered.

"I—I—I mean, the twists, and all.... I—I mean, you're all cleaned up! You— you look... pretty! Like a gay guy, I think," Brian explained.

"That's because I haven't been pitching balls to you, everyday! Besides, since when does wearing your hair in twists make you gay?!" Max asked, coming to his bed and sitting across from Brian.

"Well," Brian started, slowly. "I saw you letting that *man*, Pretty Boy, do that to you," the boy said, clearly, looking at his father.

"God! Forgive me, son! It's my fault, I should never have let you see that. I know that's something you'll never understand! .... But..."

"But, are you gay?" Brian insisted.

"Look son," Max said anxiously, and stood up. "There's a lot of things you're too young to understand.... Things about sex. You can't understand that when somebody's doing that to you... it don't matter if it's a man or a woman! I know you shouldn't have seen it... but, I didn't know you were in the building! I would never...."

"Then, that makes you bi-," Brian said, cutting him off, and answering his question.

"What?! What do you know about bi-... or gay... or any of it?!" Max asked, with the defensive confusion of the parent. "How do you know about any of that, man?"

"I know a lot, Dad," Brian said.

Now Max sat back down, and looked at his son. Brian had his face, and he was surprised at how much that face seemed to have matured since he last looked into it.

Brian looked back at him.

"I told my mama it was a lady I saw you with," he said, quietly. "I didn't want to hurt her that bad."

Now, tears began to roll down his cheeks.

"I'm sorry, son," Max said.

"She hates you," Brian added just as quietly. Then, "Where were you?! Why didn't you come and see me?! Don't you love us anymore?" Brian cried, as tears rolled down his cheeks, too.

Max moved to Brian's bed, and put his arms around his son now.

"Of course I still love you!" Max cried, hugging his boy. "I thought you didn't want to see me. I *knew* you didn't want to see me. I didn't come because I knew you didn't want to see me...."

"But, I did! I do! You're still my dad!" he cried, holding on to his father.

"God! I love you... so much! I didn't know...."

And, Max held his son for a long time that night, while they cried.

* * * * *

It was 3:30 in the morning before Max made it to his and Donnie's room.

"Whew!" he said, coming in the door trying to unhook the brace bounding him.

Donnie lay on the bed, naked. He sat up to help Max out.

"God! It's murder," he moaned, as Donnie's hands came from behind him, cupping each one.

"Oohhh... oohhh! Aaahhhh!" Max sighed, and his arms went up over his head, sandwiching his hands behind Donnie's neck. Bringing him close, he lay back on Donnie so his mouth was easily accessible, allowing his hands to massage his large, unbound breasts.

"That feel good, baby?! They feel real good! Feel good?" Donnie licked into Max's ear, and Max automatically turned to his mouth.

Donnie sent his tongue in.

"Uummm! It feels sooo good, Big Daddy.... It feels soooo good," Max moaned.

Now Donnie laid Max back on the bed. Taking a tit in each hand, he held them so that the nipples were close together.

Max gasped loudly, and arched his back in sweet anguish as Donnie took them with his teeth.

This night, Max wanted pain. He needed it to knock all the memories of his previous life —all the things he had thought about sex, love, manhood, and the guilt—out of his head. He knew he hadn't told Brian the whole truth. He knew he never could. So he felt he needed to hurt.

"Harder!" he pled, "Bite harder!" And he lay in contorted surrender, as Donnie's tongue flickered back and forth while he slowly pulled Max's throbbing nipples out between his teeth.

149

The exquisitely excruciating pain took Max's breath away, and when Donnie's teeth let go, his body trembled in convulsive shakes, leaving him anguishly gasping for air, totally, instantly pleased!

"Oh God! Oh God, Donnie!" he cried, "You hurt me so good! You hurt me soo...."

Donnie's teeth closed down hard on Max's nipples once more. He knew that he could drive Max mad at his breasts. He knew that both the pain and the pleasure seemed more intense for him there than it did even at his dick or his balls. So he let his teeth sink in ever so deeply, painfully slow. Donnie knew exactly what Max needed. He sank his teeth into his tits just deep enough and for however long it took to put Max in the zone, but never deep enough to break the skin. He was determined that for the time they had together in their room, he would keep him there in the zone.

Looking at Max's ecstagony-filled face, Donnie sank his teeth in and did it again and again.

"Oohhhh... Godddd! Bite me!" Max cried, contorting his body anguishly, sensuously. He could barely breathe while Donnie's teeth were in him. All he wanted to do was feel the pain of it, and then the exquisite eroticism when his teeth came out, and then his sucks. And with the pain and the pleasure, all the beliefs, all the thoughts, all the memories were gone—only his need for ecstagony remained.

Chapter XX

Melvin sat at a table, sipping his slow gin fizz when Donnie walked up and took a seat next to him.

"They make it the way you like it?" Donnie asked.

"Perfect," Melvin said, placing the drink on the table.

The crowd in Donnie's Place was bumping that night. Donnie had been having a good time until he spotted Melvin through the crowd. Certain he knew what the message would be, he had taken his time making his way to Melvin's table.

Pretty Boy sat at the bar, watching the whole scenario.

"Good," Donnie said, smiling. "You ready to talk?"

"That's what I came for," Melvin replied. "It's like this," he turned to Donnie. "They're asking about you and *our* man. The one I brought in. They want more of you… and Max. They say they're losing money. Customers are asking for it. They want to know where… and why you gonna go trying to stash him? They want their turns." Melvin spoke low and deliberate.

"And you've had yours," Donnie quipped, defensively before he realized it. He knew the game, but what he saw as Melvin's attitude made him angry.

"And they're saying you've had yours," Melvin replied evenly, and turned up his drink. "It's not personal with me, man," he continued, standing and bending long enough to say to Donnie: "They want you at the Lodge tomorrow night."

Then he was gone.

Donnie sat at the table alone, thinking. He knew this day would come. The way the game was set up was that a slave could go with the master whose turn it was to have him, but only for a certain period. Then he was to come back onto the market for either the next master, or if he didn't want him, to whichever master who did.

Donnie's period of time was over with Max before he took him to his cabin. Now, he knew it was Thomas Haggerty, the next master in line, who was calling for his time with Max.

But even more certain than that, now he knew he couldn't let Max go. So he was trying to decide what he was going to do to keep him.

Damn! Why does she have to be right about everything?! he thought to himself, remembering how Sharon had once told him that there was something other than Max being the best fuck, there was something more to his feelings for him.

Could it be true?! he wondered while sitting there. *Could it be true?!! And...what the fuck does that mean? What the fuck does that make me?*

Donnie didn't like to think about his past, but just then, he couldn't help himself. His mind raced.

But I didn't fuck him! it continued. *I—I just... just wanted him to stay. But...he sure as hell fucked us... didn't he? When he left. And... I ended up fucking that fat-ass mutha-fucka. Damn. Max....*

Suddenly his mind was on Max, and he remembered a conversation they had had at the desk in Max's room there at his place early on in their relationship. Max was in his robe, seated at the desk. Donnie was standing behind him, looking at him in the overhead mirror:

"Why me, man?" Max had asked. "I mean, you can fuck any of these niggas any time you want to fuck.... Why me?!"

"Why do you keep bringing it back, mutha-fucka?!" Donnie had asked, defensively. "You know what I'm gonna do... I'm gonna fuck it." He was twirling a strand of hair at the nape of Max's head, twisting it around his finger, and slowly forcing Max's head back as he sat in the chair.

Looking at himself in the mirror, back then Max knew Donnie could turn violent in an instant. Suddenly, he didn't care.

Now Donnie cupped his free hand underneath Max's chin, holding his head back and forcing his face up toward his. Very close to Max, forcing Max to look into his eyes, he whispered:

"Your ass was made for this dick, baby... it fits this dick like a glove. That's why."

Then he let his hand rub down Max's chest. Max's eyes closed as it meandered to and lingered at first one breast, and then the other.

"I can make you cum just from this alone," he whispered. Still close to Max, his fingers were squeezing the hardening nipples.

Max sat still with his eyes closed, surrendering. Only his heavy breathing was audible.

"This is really where it's at with you, baby," Donnie whispered as he continued to squeeze and massage. "That's why I'm gonna make 'em big… and juicy… and suck'em… and bite'em…"

His hands had moved down to Max's crotch, his teeth were stinging first Max's left nipple, then his right.

"…until you're soaking wet," Donnie whispered between biting nibbles.

"Mmmmm," Max moaned.

"You know I can make you cum… don't you?" Donnie asked. "Just by doing this alone," he said, and sank his teeth into Max's left nipple.

"Oohh… aahhhh!" Max sighed. "Why're you doing this to me?! Oohh… aahhhh!" he moaned, as Donnie sank his teeth in once more. "God! You're fuckin' me up! Oohhh… aahhhh! It's changing me, Big Daddy! Aahhhhh… it's fucking with my head! You're fucking with my mind…" he cried, as Donnie's teeth sank deep into first one nipple, then the other. His hand pumped Max's swollen cock until it exploded in jerky spurts onto his belly and Donnie's chin.

Max was relieved, but Donnie wasn't. His tongue crawled down Max's belly as if to lick his cum. But instead, with his hand Donnie scooped Max's cum up and, pulling him down to the floor, he rubbed it into his ass. Then, he put Max's legs over his shoulders, and holding his arms crossed over his head, cupping his chin forcing Max to look at him, he plunged into him with all his force.

"Oohhh… aaahhhhh! Dammmnn!" Max moaned.

"This is the way you like it! Don't you?!" Donnie demanded, and pushed himself deeper into him. "You want me to take you like a bitch… 'cause… deep down… you know you got a bit of bitch in you… don't you?!"

"Noooo," Max moaned.

"Don't you?!" Donnie growled. He was all the way into Max now. "You love the dick… don't you?! Don't you?!" he demanded, banging Max so hard, it felt and sounded like he was punching him.

"Noooo! Yesss… yessss!" Max cried out of pleasure, pain and fear. "Yes, Big Daddy!"

153

"Then, tell me you love it, bitch," Donnie demanded. "Tell me you love the dick...."

"I love it, Big Daddy! I love it! I love the dick...."

"Keep saying it, mutha-fuckin' bitch! You're not gonna be able to fuck butter when I'm through with your ass tonight, baby! Keep sayin'.... Aahhh! Whoaa!!! Good ass, baby! This some good ass!" Donnie groaned as his cum exploded so powerfully into Max, it pushed him out.

They both lay there on the floor, on their backs, breathing heavily and holding each others hand. Each totally satisfied and amazed at how good they felt.

* * * * *

"Give him to them, Donnie!"

He heard Pretty Boy before he realized he was sitting at the table next to him.

"What the hell you talking about?!" Donnie's murmur was threatening.

"I'm talking about that hypocritical, low-down, down-low mutha-fucka you got up at the cabin!"

Donnie knocked the chair over when he angrily stood up. It had taken everything in him to keep from socking Pretty Boy, himself.

"Leave it alone, bitch.... Leave it alone," he hissed low enough so that only Pretty Boy could hear him. Then he stormed off through the crowd.

Now Pretty Boy was the one who sat there alone, thinking.

From the scene, Pretty Boy knew who Soledad was. His surprise came when he learned that they were in the same city. All his life he dreamed of meeting the man who would accept him for what he was. A man who would watch over him, protect and love him. He had dreamed of giving Soledad head ever since he first laid eyes on that 13 inch cock fucking some white kid on the back of a truck in video a few years earlier.

Now Soledad lay naked, face down, on a mat on the floor in the eastern room at the spa where Pretty Boy did part-time work, waiting for him.

Soft Asian music was playing in the background when Pretty Boy came through the sliding wood-framed doors, dressed in a kimono. He was a pretty man.

Dancing around the room exotically, erotically, and without saying a word, Pretty Boy came out of the kimono as he came closer to where Donnie lay. Underneath, he wore a flap tied to a leather string around his waist. Nothing else covered his light, smooth, beautifully-androgynous body.

On his knees, straddling Donnie, Pretty Boy laid his chest to Donnie's back, stretching his arms out as far as they could go.

Then Donnie felt his wet, hot tongue. First his left ear... then licking and kissing Donnie's bald head around and over to his right. Then at the back of his neck, and slowly down his back, licking and kissing and sucking every inch. Finally, down to his buns, and on to his silky, puckered ass.

Pretty Boy used his tongue to lick and suck around and around until it hit bull's eye and he sent it into the wet, puckered, tight hole again and again.

"Uuhhh! Uuhhh! Uuhhh!" Donnie sighed each time.

When the beautiful Pretty Boy realized Donnie couldn't take anymore and would soon explode, he stopped, and lifting his leg over his head, he turned him over.

The first time Donnie laid eyes on Pretty Boy, he was awed by his beauty. He was the prettiest man he had ever seen. Then, his looks, coupled with his tongue, had him as hard as he had ever been.

Pretty Boy's hands were beneath Donnie's hard ass, grasping his cheeks in a way that made it look as if he was serving himself Donnie's balls. After licking and nibbling his way from Donnie's ass, across the base of him, Pretty Boy's hot mouth closed in on his balls. Now he lay on his belly, prostrated between Donnie's legs, sucking his balls and humming in time with the soft, music surrounding them. The thumb on one hand massaged Donnie's base, his other hand squeezed and massaged the head of Donnie's huge, hard cock.

Every now and then, Pretty Boy could hear Donnie sigh. To Pretty Boy Donnie looked and felt like he was floating in his hands, laying there with his eyes closed tight. He felt good and determined he would keep him satisfied.

In actuality that night as Donnie lay there with his eyes closed, he had gone to another place. As he lay there being orally-serviced by Pretty Boy, in his mind he had gone back to his darkened bedroom over 15 years ago. And it was his stepfather, who himself had been a pretty man, if fat, whose mouth and hands were servicing him—consuming him.

It was the first time his stepfather had stolen into his bedroom and awakened him like that.

Aahhh...aahhh... aaahhhh! Aahhh! Fuck! This why this mutha-fucka gave me that shit!!! Donnie remembered thinking, too plastered to the ecstasy and the bed to fight him off. He was rock-hard and wasted, and his mother was at his ailing grandparents'.

Now, his stepfather was sucking the head of his huge rod. It was the first time anyone had ever done that to him, and a hot heat like nothing he had never felt before consumed him.

Holding Donnie's foreskin back with one hand and the base of his cock with the other, his stepfather sent the tip of his tongue into the slit, then closed his wet, hot mouth down taking in as much of him as he could.

Next the man put Vaseline on Donnie's cock, and rubbed some into his own ass, as he straddled his stepson, and forced himself down onto the helplessly hard, waiting dick!

Out of his head with the erotic insanity of thinking about that, it wasn't until Donnie felt the blood on his hands did he come back to that first night with Pretty Boy, to find him bleeding, cowering in a corner of the disheveled, Asian room!

"I didn't mean to fuck you up like that, man," Donnie said, having come to his senses. He handed a five years younger Pretty Boy a drink. They were in the kitchen at his place. "You can't suck a nigga's shit like that, and expect to walk away! Shit!" Donnie said, pulling at his crotch, "I mean... I would have tried to fuck a tree if one had been there, man, after that tongue!"

Pretty Boy was recuperating at Donnie's after being released from the hospital. He'd spent three days there with packing and sutures after his first encounter with Donnie.

"So I want you here... here, baby," Donnie was massaging Pretty Boy's shoulders. "You won't have nothing to worry about...." Donnie was whispering in Pretty Boy's ear like he would later do to Max, many times. "I'm gonna take care of you—and that tongue... 'cause I want to feel it every mutha-fuckin' day!"

Pretty Boy had been with Donnie ever since.

That's the way it was with us... Pretty Boy thought. *...until Max!*

And, he made up his mind that night, sitting at the empty table at Donnie's Place, that no matter what he had to do, he wouldn't lose Donnie, and he wouldn't let Donnie lose everything. He was determined that not Max, but he was the one who would always be with Donnie.

He finished his drink. Then, he picked up the chair Donnie knocked over and carefully placed it and his own chair back up to the table. He threw his hair back and followed Donnie through the crowd.

He knew what he felt he had to do.

Chapter XXI

A few days later, Donnie was back at his cabin, in bed with Max.

"Hummmm… mmmmm…. Aahhhh… I love this ass, baby," Donnie moaned as he rhythmically slapped his pelvis against Max's ass, his engorged cock buried in him, as they lay together on their sides. Donnie was taking Max his favorite way, undulating slow and easy, he was in him as deep as he could go. "You like this dick, baby? You like this big-ass cock?!"

"Mmmmm…" Max was moaning too. "I love it, Big Daddy," he cried, arching his ass the way he knew Donnie loved, and pressing himself back against Donnie, giving him maximum exposure. "I love it… I love it… I love you… Donnie! I love you!" Max sighed with each thrust.

"Aaahhhhh!" Donnie cried, and exploded with such uncontrollable force it sent his body into an anguished contortion of tormented delight. "You love this dick, baby! You love this dick!" he replied, when he could.

Feeling the heat of Donnie's fiery liquid filling his bowels, Max moaned as he felt his own liquids explode onto his belly and the sheet beneath him.

"Don-nie! Don-nie! Oh God! I love you! You hurt me so good… and I love it! I love you."

It was the first time Max had called Donnie's name, telling him he loved him during their love-making. It caught Donnie off guard.

"Mmmmm, good ass, baby," Donnie sighed, breathing deeply, satisfied. "My dick loves your ass," he added, and pulled away from Max, lying back on the pillow with one hand behind his head, he was massaging his cock with the other.

Now Max turned to him. Pulling himself up onto him, he brought his leg up so that Donnie's cock rested beneath his thigh. He used his thigh to massage it, keeping it there. He turned Donnie's smiling lips to his own and sent his tongue into Donnie's mouth.

"I love you," Max said softly, looking at him. "I don't know why you chose me… why you *made* me…. But you made me!" He sent his tongue into Donnie's mouth again. "And now… I love you…." He lightly sucked Donnie's bottom lip. "I don't think I've ever loved anybody the way I love you," Max said honestly.

Kissing, now Donnie lay Max down on his back.

He knew Pretty Boy was on his way to pick him up soon. But he had been to the Lodge and he knew what they wanted. He also knew what he wanted. He had to keep Max. So he had developed a plan. A plan he was ready to implement.

What he, nor Max, knew was that Pretty Boy was just outside the bedroom door.

"Do you love me?!" he asked, taking Max's growing breasts in his hands and forcing his nipples together. He took them into his mouth before Max could reply.

"Mmm! Mmmm Uummmmm!" Max moaned, ecstatically. "I... love... you...."

Not letting go, "Do you?!" Donnie asked through gently clenched teeth.

"Goddd! Yes!" Max sighed sensuously. "I love you... I love you...."

"Then, prove it!" Donnie said, still squeezing, licking and sucking Max's nipples.

"What do you want me to do, Don-nie? I'll do anything! Anything!"

"You'll do anything?!" Donnie asked, continuing his erotic torment.

"Yesss! Goddd... yesss!! I love you... tell me.... Aahhhh! Tell me what you want me to do! I'll do anything you want...."

"Be a woman... become a woman. Be my woman, baby," Donnie said, clearly, plainly, simply.

It took several silent seconds before Max realized what he said—what he meant. And when the reality of his words sank in, Max had to take in several deep breaths before he could say anything.

"Wha...?!! What?! What do you mean?! What are you saying?!" he asked, breathlessly from both Donnie's words as well as from what he was doing to him.

"You're halfway there," Donnie said, and sucked his nipples hard. "I want you to go all the way, baby.... I want you to become my woman."

"Goddd! Goddd!" Max exclaimed, shocked. Pulling away from him, "I can't!!! Don't ask me to do that! Goddd! Donnie! I'm a man...."

"Damn! I know what you are!" Donnie said through tightly clenched teeth.

Max's nipples stung. He pulled away.

"Just don't say you love me...."

"I do love you... Donnie.... Please! Look at me!" Max cried on his knees beside Donnie on the bed, cupping his breasts. The wet, glistening breasts Donnie had been sucking seconds ago. "I did this for you! I let... I want you to fuck me whenever you want... whenever you will.... I don't want anybody else! I just want you...."

"You love this dick, baby! That's what you love!" Donnie spate the words at him. "You love it when it's fucking your fucking brains out! But you don't love me."

Pretty Boy peeped as Donnie reached over and took the tray from the nightstand, and snorted a row of coke.

"I love you, Donnie!" Max pleaded, rubbing his leg. "Don't ask me to do that! I'm a man! I have a son! Goddd! I love you... but... I can't!"

"You say you love me, but you won't be my woman!"

"I am.. your woman! For all intents and purposes, Donnie! I am your woman!" Max cried.

"Do you want to be with me?" Donnie demanded.

"You know I do—you made me this way, Donnie! Damn! You made me like this! I don't... I can't be with anybody else—I love you...."

"Then..." Donnie started, sitting up and pulling Max into his arms, "...be my woman. It's the only way we can be together, baby...." he said, gently.

"Why?!" Max asked. "Why?" he pled.

Donnie turned Max's face to his.

"I told you I had to go to the Lodge.... *They* called me! And it wasn't to fuck, Max. It was because they want you!—You and me. And then you'll go to the next one"

Donnie could see the surprise in Max's face.

"They've seen you, baby. And they liked what they saw.... And, with these," he cupped Max's breasts, "they'll want you even more." He saw the tears in Max's eyes.

Pretty Boy watched as Donnie kissed them away, lovingly, still cupping Max's breasts.

"I can't put you back out there," Donnie whispered, and kissed Max again. "You see, I do love your ass! Damn, baby! I don't know how that happened... it wasn't supposed to...."

Hearing Donnie say the word, suddenly Max pressed his lips to his.

"You love me?! You do love me!" Max was laughing through his tears. "You said you love me... and... that's all that matters," he cried, filling Donnie's face and throat with wet, tear-stained kisses. "I love you so much! I don't want to be with anybody else.... Donnie... I want to be with you.... I want to be with you!"

And when he felt Donnie sucking, nibbling, licking, biting:

"I'll be whatever you want, Donnie—anything you want!" he cried. "God! I'll do whatever you want! I'll be anything you want, Don-nie!" he cried in total submission and surrender to Donnie!

Pretty Boy backed away from the door. Having seen, heard and felt enough of their love, he didn't need to know anything else. So, pushing his long curly hair back behind his ears, he held his hands there to block out the sounds of their love as he slowly, quietly backed off down the hall to the kitchen.

When the deed was done, he then went to the car to wait for Donnie.

A little while later, Donnie stood over the sink spitting out the tomato juice he had just drank. Max came in just in time to see him spitting out the red liquid.

"Damn!" Donnie spate out the word while pouring the carton of tomato juice down the drain. "That's why I hate this shit! It tastes like crap!"

At first Max had been alarmed. Now, clad in a short, satin robe, he came to Donnie with a paper towel.

"I put liquor in it before I drink it," he said, drying the corners of Donnie's mouth with a paper towel. "Who knows how long it's been in there... it's probably spoiled," Max concluded with a peck on Donnie's lips. "Now, tell me one more time how we're gonna do this," he said, standing close to Donnie, Max was holding Donnie's arms around his waist.

Donnie felt as sure about what he had asked, and Max had agreed, to do than he had about anything in a long time. He was as sure about Max as he was about anyone he had ever known. The love they had been making minutes ago was the best sex he could ever remember having—but it was always great with Max. Soon, he would have absolute proof of Max's love. And he was going to take it.

"Remember, I'll be at the Lodge all next week. So, lay low. I'll take care of everything from there...." He kissed Max full on the lips while loosening his grip and escaping. He grabbed his bag off a chair by the door. "Good thing you got your passport," he said. "We'll fly to Brazil...."

Again, Max joined him, smiling. They kissed.

"Or maybe Thailand... I'm not sure. I'll find out, and I'll call you from there."

Again, they kissed.

"Just... be ready." Donnie turned. "Be ready for me, baby," he said.

And then he was gone.

Chapter XXII

Max hung up the telephone, disappointed that Donnie would be very late coming to the cabin. "Keep it hot for me, baby," Donnie had said, "I'll be there no matter how long this takes."

It had been more than a week since he and Donnie had been together, and now he was beginning to be suspicious that perhaps Donnie had met someone else. He knew Donnie had gone back to the Lodge, recently. But Donnie had said he loved him and that he wanted him to stay there every time they talked. So he tried not to let his mind dwell on his suspicions.

He poured himself another glass of wine, took a sip, and then he snorted a row of the cocaine he had prepared for Donnie. Sitting on the side of the bed, he rubbed Donnie's pillow and rubbed himself, thinking about Donnie. He wanted... no, he needed to see him... be with him.

I'll rent a car and surprise him! No... suppose I miss him coming here? God, he thought, bringing his hand up to his breast. Bringing them together like Donnie always did, he was squeezing and pulling his nipples hard. He lay back on the bed. *He's got to come,* he thought. "Gooddd!" he moaned, feeling his semen wetting his pants, "he's got to come!" He lay there waiting for his breathing to return to normal, before he sat up and turned up his glass of wine.

Holding his wetness away from himself, he went into the bathroom, turned on the shower, removed his pants and stepped in. With the water pouring down on him, his mind was filled with thoughts of Donnie. He remembered the first time he caught a glimpse of him in the bathroom at his gym that sunny Sunday afternoon, that first day he and Brian had come. Now he realized he had desired him even then, and that desire had led him back in the shower to secretly quench it.

"God, he's got to come," he said, stepping out of the shower, he stood looking at his wet, naked body in the mirror. The full breasts—merely seeing Donnie's eyes on them could practically make Max cum—the now limp cock that Donnie no longer wanted him to have. Reaching behind himself, he grabbed it and tucked it and his balls between his legs; he had to see what Donnie would see. His loose, wet hair falling down to his shoulders, his protruding breasts, to himself he looked almost feminine, save for the shadow of a mustache. *The hormones are doing their job,* he thought.

After he dried himself, he went to the medicine cabinet and removed his razor. The mustache was gone in less than 5 minutes. He thought about how pleased Donnie would be to kiss him without feeling the hair on his lip. The thought made him smile at himself in the mirror, pleased. He would get the electrolysis soon.

Still naked, he took a new bottle of baby oil from the cabinet underneath the sink, and going back to the bedroom, he placed it on the nightstand beside the bed. Pouring himself another glass of wine, he drank it. He poured another and set it on the nightstand, too. Then he bent over and snorted another row of cocaine. Next, sitting on the side of the bed, he oiled his whole body, rubbing the oil in until he was glistening. He thought about how much Donnie was going to love touching him when he crawled into the warm, snug bed and cuddled up behind him later that night, like he had done so many nights before.

He could hardly wait.

He was feeling good now. And though it was early in the evening, it was dark outside. He clicked on the lamp. Opening the drawer on the nightstand, he removed the jar and 2 tablets. He swallowed the hormones, chasing them with wine. Placing the jar back in the drawer, he removed a sealed packet, tore it open and removed the plastic syringe. He filled it with baby oil. Then he turned the lamp off. Falling back onto the bed and spreading his legs, there in the dark, Max inserted the syringe into his anus and slowly pressed down, like he had done to himself so many times before, until the syringe was empty.

Reaching, he placed the empty syringe on the nightstand. Then Max pulled the covers up to his chin and quickly fell into a deep, drug-induced sleep.

* * * * *

Donnie counted out $60,000 cash as Pretty Boy drove them back from the Lodge. He had performed for the camera every chance he got while they were there—determined to get the money for his and Max's trip—and for Max's surgery. Now he had enough.

"More than enough," Donnie said.

He handed Pretty Boy $5,000. Then he put the other money in his duffle.

"What are you gonna do?" Pretty Boy asked, watching him suspiciously out of the corner of his eyes.

"Don't get in my business," Donnie said, firing up a joint.

"What about us?!" Pretty Boy asked, after Donnie took a couple of deep tokes on the joint.

"What do you mean, what about us?!" Donnie asked. "You know what it is with us, baby-bo…" a cough cut Donnie off! "Damn! You see what you did to me?!" he was beating his chest, clearing his throat. " Asking me some crazy shit like that!" he said.

"You don't look too good," Pretty Boy said, looking at Donnie.

Just then the headlights of a car traveling in the opposite direction came out of the night, shining it's lights in their faces.

Donnie was sweating.

Pretty Boy had to swerve to keep control of the car!

"Look at the mutha-fuckin' road, baby-boy! Get us home… not killed!" Donnie laughed, surprised that he would choke over some reefer. He took another deep draw on the joint, and immediately his chest filled and coughs spilled from him.

"No… Donnie, you really don't look too good," Pretty Boy insisted.

"Stay out of my fucking business," Donnie said.

He put the joint in the tray, and pulling his collar up he turned away from Pretty Boy, and dozed off.

He's never been a sweater… Pretty Boy thought while driving along in the dark. Working around sick people, he knew what to look for. *But Donnie's the healthiest person I know!* Still, he couldn't help thinking about the sweating. He first noticed it while they were at the Lodge. *A cold, maybe… 'cause he's never sick!* Pretty Boy thought, consoling himself, refusing to think of any other cause.

* * * * *

Was he dreaming when he felt the bed shake and now feeling his hot body snuggling in close behind, joining him in the fetal position? He felt his arm go beneath him, the other around him. One caressing his cock, the other cupping his balls.

"Aahhhh… Don-nie," he sighed, feeling his hot breath on his neck, his hard rod immediately behind him.

He wasn't dreaming. This was real.

He pushed his ass back anxious to receive it, but it didn't happen.

Instead, his hands were all over him, as if taking in the firm, smoothness of his body for the first time. He felt good knowing how silky the oil made him feel on the sheets. He knew it made him feel good to his hands.

He felt his hands move to his breasts, the breasts he loved, and his own hands went up to hold them there, pressing his entire body back against him.

"Ooohhhh, baby!" he whispered, "I love you, Donnie! I want you! I want it!"

And in that instant, he felt the head of the huge hardness he felt he knew so well enter.

"Mmmmm... it feels so good," Max cried.

"Yeessss, Maxie.... Yeessss!" came the reply.

So engrossed in the feeling, Max didn't notice that for the first time he had called him by his full name. And when all of his cock was into his oil-oozing anus, and his deep thrusting began, nothing else on earth mattered to Max. He was in the zone for the rest of the night.

Before daybreak the next morning, Max reached behind him for Donnie's arm, and brought it around underneath his own arm, to his breast.

But his arm didn't feel right!

"Who are you?!" Max demanded, jumping up from the bed in surprise when he saw that the arm was hairy and white, and it belonged to Tom, not Donnie!

"You'll know soon enough," Tom said. "Now, come back to bed." He was lifting the covers for Max.

"You... you'd better get the hell out of here!" Max hissed. "Donnie?!" he called over his shoulder, while keeping an eye on Tom, who let the covers fall and lay back with his hands behind his head.

"Donnie?!" Max called again even louder, backing toward the door.

"Who the hell you calling?" Tom asked, amused.

"Somebody who's gonna kick your ass!" Max said, and opened the door, calling: "Don....!" He stopped, shocked to see two, huge guys, one white, one black, standing just outside the bedroom door!

"Come on back to bed, Maxie," Tom called. And suddenly Max realized it had been Tom who had made love to him the night before.

He was bewildered.

Then a fear and a dread entered him like none he had ever known as, naked, he backed back into the room, and closed the door. It made him feel faint, and he leaned his back against the door to support himself.

"What have you done with..." he had to swallow. "Where's Donnie?" he asked, almost in a whisper.

Tom lay looking at him.

"Donnie? Donnie? Oohhh!" Tom chuckled. "You mean, Soledad! Big Daddy! I see where it had gotten to between you and Donnie Soledad Williams!" This time he laughed. "Here I am thinking you're saying 'Daddy' last night, and all the while you're saying 'Donnie! I love you, Donnie!'" he mimicked Max.

Max could see that he was really amused, but Tom's amusement did nothing to alleviate his own fear and dread, and now, confusion.

"I mean Donnie!" Max almost screamed. "Donnie!" he yelled. "Donnie!" he said, softly, his eyes filling with tears.

Tom could see the anguish in his face and body, as he lay back against the door. He remembered reading the poems Max had written to Donnie. The poems that had caused him to publish the book. The poems that had made him want Max for himself. Tom sat up, now. He placed the covers over his nakedness.

"Soledad..." he started, slowly. "Donnie's not here, Max. I'm Tom... Tom Haggerty," he looked at Max and could see the tears roll down the sides of his face. Coming to Max, he lifted his chin and wiped the tears away. "You belong to me now," he continued.

"Nooo!" Max sobbed, turning away. "Donnie wouldn't do that! Not now! Where is he," breathless, "Plea-see! Where is he?!" He wanted to move. He tried to, but his broken heart wouldn't let him.

As Tom Haggerty stood there, Max slid down to the floor and lay there in a crumbled huddle, sobbing deeply.

Chapter XXIII

Pretty Boy's concern had not been unfounded that night, three months ago, when he drove Donnie back from the Lodge. When they got back that night, Donnie had gone straight to his bedroom. And, try as he might, Pretty boy couldn't shake the feeling.

He unpacked the SUV, and put everything away. It was when he went to Donnie's bedroom to see if he needed anything did he find Donnie packing a suitcase, to his surprise.

"Where are you going?" coming into the room, Pretty Boy asked, suspiciously.

"Sharon…. She'll be running the Lodge," Donnie said to Pretty Boy, while hurriedly almost nervously packing, Pretty Boy thought.

"Where are you going?!" he asked again, and this time it sounded more like a demand.

"You don't need to know where I'm going," Donnie answered. "Just.. run everything by her, first, okay?"

"Okay."

"And—and keep me posted…. Call everyday…."

"But, Donnie!" Pretty Boy cut him off, "I want to know where you're gonna be!"

Donnie slammed the suitcase top down.

"Are you in this with me?" Donnie asked. "Are you here for me?!" he insisted, turning to Pretty Boy.

"You know it! You know I am! But… Donnie… Donnie…."

"Then, stay the fuck out of my business!" Donnie said, turning to lift the suitcase from the bed.

In the same instant, the suitcase and its entire contents fell to the floor, as Donnie turned, sweating! Without saying a word, he staggered. Then his eyes rolled back into his head and he too fell like a man who had just received a knock-out punch!

Pretty Boy stood outside the emergency room, biting his manicured nails, when Sharon came rushing in.

"What's wrong?!" she asked, coming up to him. "What happened to him?"

Pretty Boy hunched his shoulders.

"They won't tell me nothing," he said, without taking his eyes off the team of doctors around an unconscious Donnie who was on the emergency room table with IVs in each arm.

"Donnie!" Sharon said softly, touching the glass. "Is Dr. Stewart here? Has he gotten here, yet?"

"They drew some blood," Pretty Boy whispered. "He's walking it through testing."

"Oh God!" Sharon cried.

Just then, they saw Donnie turn his head, abruptly. They watched as the doctors on each side of him grasped his arms, tightly, to keep him from moving them. They watched as Donnie opened his eyes, looking at the doctors and nurses about him almost in horrified disbelief. They couldn't hear Donnie when he said to them:

"I've got to get to Max!"

But, Pretty Boy read his lips, correctly.

* * * * *

After three months with Thomas, Max no longer dressed unless Thomas told him to do so. And then, you had to look extremely close to tell whether he was male or female. Thomas made certain that he had electrolysis, and had seen to it that he learned how to make up his face. He wanted him to, and taught him how to play up his androgyny.

With Thomas, he had become the poet he had secretly always dreamed of becoming. His book of poems was out there on the circuit, and so were he and Thomas. Traveling to events all over the country where he would be called upon to give a reading. Usually, in a darkened room, under a spotlight, sitting on a barstool, with his legs crossed. Naked, except for the leather collar he always wore around his neck, the strap on it was usually held by Thomas, who stood nearby, in the shadows.   With Thomas, if nothing else, Max learned how the game the boys at the Lodge played, was played.   With Thomas, Max learned what it meant to be a slave.

"I like it here, Dad. I want to stay here at Hargrove's," Brian had said, when Thomas let Max stop by the school to tell his son he was moving to New York.

Thomas and his boys had Max's gear already packed and lodged in the limousine when they came to the cabin to get him. He had decided that driving to New York would give him a chance to get to know Max, up close and personal. And he did several times on that drive.

At first Max couldn't believe Donnie had actually sold him. For a solid month he cried, and tried to call Donnie to tell him how much he hated him for what he had done every chance he got. But he was never able to get through. The closest he ever got were the two times when he spoke with Pretty Boy who had told him: *Donnie don't want yo'ass no more—leave us alone, crazy-ass bitch!* or, *Get a life, bitch—you're cracking up! And leave us alone!* Then the line would go dead. Finally he called and the operator said the account had been changed to an unpublished number. He wrote letters, but still there was no reply. The only way he could see Donnie was on video. So he scoured the internet for every video he and Donnie had made, and he would spend every waking second when he was alone watching them.

Finally the day came when Max thought — *That mutha-fucka didn't care! Turn you out... and then... leave... sell you. Love you?!* The thought almost made him laugh out loud and he feared he really would lose his mind. *He never loved you,* he thought. *If anything... he hated yo'ass!*

The first time he thought that, tears swelled up in his eyes, and slowly ran down his face.

And look at you, his mind said to him in disgust, as he wiped the tears away with the back of his hands. *You punk-ass mutha-fucka—you still love his ass! You punk-ass mutha-fucka!*

Max did still love Donnie.

No matter how much he wanted to hate him, he couldn't. So in his mind, he decided that his present life—his life with Thomas Haggerty—was his penitence for all the people he had let down in his old life. And he wore his penitence well, silently taking every abuse and graciously taking the acclaim of being a published poet. He was on the verge of becoming a celebrity on the circuit, but he didn't care. Jaded, Max didn't care about too much of anything, anymore.

Still, sometimes he missed Donnie so much he felt he couldn't get high enough to wipe thoughts of him out of his head. Those were the times when he would let his mind run forward to an imaginary time when they would meet in Bangkok for his surgery.

In his mind, he and Donnie lay together in bed. This would be the last time they would make love together—man on man. He could feel Donnie's hands all over him, touching and squeezing everything. And his mouth. His wet, hot mouth! Now his teeth, and the wonderfully sweet pain.

"Donnie!" he always whispered and ended up crying.

Thomas had caught him crying Donnie's name several times before. It was usually after those times when he would put Max in the collar and hurt him.

The first time, he had let his two guards, in prison guard uniforms beat, and then run a train on the prisoner-clad Max—collared, handcuffed, bleeding, thrown over an A-frame, with his pants hanging down around his ankles. Thomas had two cameras videotaping and streaming the action.

Though Max's pelvis was sore for days, he had taken his penitence stoically, refusing to cry out and refusing to ask for mercy.

While at first Thomas seemed to marvel in taking Max everywhere in his collar, showing him off with his boobs and his book. Now three months had passed, and to Max it seemed the novelty of his poetic license was wearing off Thomas. He used to dress and make Max up androgynously so that they would get all the attention, as they strolled through the park. Now sometimes, Max felt like he despised him. He had given up trying to adjust to Thomas's bizarre, exhibitionist sexual needs. For the last three months, Max was simply taking whatever drugs he could get his hands on to keep his mind off Donnie, and to take whatever Tom was dishing out.

So that evening in early spring when Thomas swung into Max's room without his bodyguards, Max's initial thought was not why he had come.

"It's been a beautiful day," Thomas said, going to Max's closet. He came out with a 2-piece black cashmere sweat-suit and the trench he had bought for him.

"Get dressed. Make yourself up! Let's go for a walk, Maxie," Thomas ordered.

He watched as Max went to his dressing table, sat down, and with make-up, changed from looking almost like a man to looking totally like a woman.

171

When he was finished, Thomas was pleased.

* * * * *

Max failed to notice anything out of the ordinary late that evening as he and Thomas walked through the park together. Thomas was always stopping and chatting with people about their children and their pets. So, for him not to have noticed and approached the men with the large, grey, Great Dane that evening, would have been out of the ordinary. Max had stood off, like he usually did, allowing Thomas his few minutes to greet and admire, and then they would move on.

But, shortly after moving on that evening, Max began to feel that old familiar haze, like he had been slipped a Mickey, starting to overtake him. Immediately he knew that it was whatever had been in the flask Thomas handed him, and it was already taking affect.

"Getting chilly! This will keep you warm," he said, handing Max the flask from which he himself had just feigned a swallow.

Max took it and turned it up.

Now they were in a part of the park Max had never seen before. His head was spinning, and Thomas could no longer hold him up.

Suddenly he found himself practically being carried deep into the woods. Men— maybe 7 or 8 of them, he thought—were carrying him into the woods. A clearing, small and tight.... And the breathing... loud! Panting... up close!

He wanted to ask: *What's happening?! Why? Where's Tom?* But the words couldn't come out.

He felt first his shoes... then his pants come off. And the panting... loud... up close!

And he knew.

God-damn! he moaned as the oil-filled syringe entered.

He could only moan, as he felt himself being placed face down and held over what felt like a small boulder covered with blankets.... And... the panting... loud... close!

It was the Great Dane!

He felt the huge beast's cold nose sniffing, and hot, rough, wet tongue licking his ass! He felt the huge beast hovering over his back, hunching up on its hind legs and using its front paws to crawl up and hold onto the blankets over the boulder, as its masters guided his ready, massively-extended meat into Max's ass!

This can't be happening! Goddd! Nooo! This isn't happening to me! Max was crying out in his mind.

"Noooo!"

He knew it was happening. He knew he was being screwed by the huge dog! He knew Thomas had planned it, and, was filming it all. And he knew he could do nothing but take it.

But, even as he felt the warmth from the beast on his back, and it's powerful, quick, undulating pumping inside him, Max knew he had let it go too far.

Chapter XXIV

Three months ago, Dr. Marc Stewart stood in Donnie's hospital room waiting for them with the results of his blood tests. Pretty Boy walked with Sharon, a doctor and attendants as they came off the elevator pushing a gurney Donnie was on to his hospital room to find Dr. Stewart, waiting.

As the attendants lifted Donnie onto the bed, Pretty Boy hung back, watching intensely.

Pretty Boy knew what it had come down to before Dr. Stewart said a word. Staring at Donnie, he watched the attendants leave the room. As Sharon asked questions, he stared at Donnie as the doctors exchanged many words he had heard before at the hospice. Words like: *'recently contracted,' 'a particularly virulent strain,' 'full-blown.'* And to him it seemed that Donnie was staring back at him. Pretty Boy knew Donnie had HIV/AIDS.

And with that knowledge, he felt his world closing down around him.

He didn't remember how he had made it to the hospital chapel. He only remembered finding himself there, on his knees, praying: "Dear God! Dear God... not Donnie! Not Donnie! I'll do anything! Anything! Take me... but, don't take Donnie from me! P-l-e-a-s-e!"

He didn't remember how long he knelt there, crying, praying and vowing to do penance. Before he left he had vowed that he would take care of Donnie, that he would be there for Donnie, that he would never leave Donnie—and Donnie would never leave him.

* * * * *

Donnie didn't talk much that first month when he learned he had AIDS. He was only in the hospital for 4 days that first time. When he came to, his mind was on Max. He knew he could never tell him; and he knew he would never be able to make love to him the way he wanted to make love to him, again. Yet, more than anything, he wanted to feel himself sinking all the way into Max just one more time. And he knew he would do it as soon as they were together.

Max loves me... totally, he thought. *He trusts me. He'd be willing to give it up!* Then, in the next breath, *I can't do this to him.*

So, as soon as he got home, he telephoned the publisher, Thomas Haggerty.

He had given Max's book of poems to Tom when he had been called to the Lodge. And Tom had shown a lot of interest in his poems, and, in Max. He knew he would gladly take Max away.

In giving Max away, Donnie knew he would spend the rest of his life missing him, wanting him, and loving him.

Then one evening when the fever had hold of Donnie in the worst way, he and Pretty Boy were alone in his bedroom like before. The drugs had Donnie feeling certain he was lucid and in control, but Pretty Boy knew he was losing it.

"I've got to go!" Donnie said suddenly, standing up, wobbly. He laughed, thinking it was due to the liquor he and Pretty Boy had been drinking and the other drugs they had been taking.

Pretty Boy jumped up to catch him.

"Where are you going, Donnie?" he asked, trying to steady Donnie and make him sit back down.

"You know where... to the cabin!" Donnie said, pulling away from him. "Max's waiting.... I promised him I'd come... cum!" He laughed at his naughtiness, and stumbled toward the door.

Pretty Boy realized the delirium had sent Donnie's mind back three months ago to the night when the illness first overtook him, and Donnie thought he was getting ready to go to the cabin to Max. Pretty Boy hated it. He hated himself— but he hated Max even more for being off in the world, enjoying his life, he felt.

"Max's ass ain't there, Donnie! You need to go to bed!" He was after him, trying to force him back.

But, being that ill, Donnie still had enough guile to fake Pretty Boy out, getting around him.

"I will," he said, grabbing the jacket with his car keys in the pocket. "He's waiting for me... in bed!"

He disappeared through the door.

"Damn him!" Pretty Boy said, scrambling to his feet. "Damn him!"

Donnie had started the Mercedes by the time Pretty Boy, on his heels, opened the door and jumped in on the passenger side.

"Let me drive, Donnie! You don't need to be driving," he urged.

It had gotten this far before. And like before, Pretty Boy figured he'd drive Donnie around until he went to sleep—or passed out. Then he would drive him back home like before.

But Donnie was already backing out of the driveway onto the street, burning rubber!

"At least, slow down!" Pretty Boy shrieked. But Donnie couldn't hear him. All he could hear was the poisonous blood coursing threw his veins. All he could feel was his body needing what his mind could no longer stop him from going after.

"The red light! The red light!" Pretty Boy yelled, as Donnie drove through it, and then, the next one too.

Sweat was pouring from both their brows—Donnie's from the fever, Pretty Boy's from fear. He decided to sit back and be quiet as they sped out of the city.

I deserve this, he thought, looking at Donnie. He thought about all the years he had been with Donnie, and how many times he had wanted Donnie to take him forcibly again after that first time — *if that's the way you want to get it!* he thought. But Donnie never did, not the way he had taken Max.

Now he contented himself with the thought: *I'll be there when you see that that bastard couldn't care less about you! I'm the one who's here! I've been here! God! I didn't... I didn't...."*

Donnie's head was filled with thoughts of how good he would feel crawling in bed behind Max, like all the times before, the prelude to what was to follow. Max's warm and clean nakedness, his sweet smell, how he would moan when he felt his hands on him, the way he would feel in his mouth, and in his body.

"I love you, Donnie... " he heard Max sigh.

"I love... ya... Max!" Donnie stammered in reply to his delusion.

Hearing Donnie say Max's name, something suddenly snapped in Pretty Boy.

"Damn you!" he growled, startling Donnie back to the moment. "Damn Max!" he continued. "I hate him!"

"Don't... say that...." Donnie murmured, shaking.

176

"I do," Pretty Boy said, reaching to wipe the sweat from Donnie's brow.

Donnie pushed his hand away. And in that motion, it seemed, all the anger, hate and jealousy Pretty Boy had ever felt about Donnie's love for Max exploded in him.

"I hate him!" he repeated, and his voice had taken on a tone Donnie had never heard come from him before—it was a deadly tone.

Donnie tried to look at him, swerving the SUV as he did; he had to fight to straighten it up. But this time, Pretty Boy wasn't fazed.

"It was supposed to be him!" he said, evenly. "You're dying... and it was supposed to be him!" he said, pulling his staring eyes from the road, looking at Donnie. "And... you protected him! Damn you! You sent him away to protect him! But... I stayed.... I take care of you... I suck your cock, Donnie... knowing! Goodddd! I don't care! I wanna die... if you die.... 'Cause... *I* love you! Oh God! How I love you!"

For an instant, Donnie wondered was he hallucinating. He had never heard Pretty Boy talk like this. He had never heard Pretty Boy say he loved him. He tried to look at him, as well as he tried to look at the road and control the SUV.

"But you never saw me! You... never cared! You never saw anybody after Max! All you ever saw was Max... and... I hate him!" Pretty Boy was crying now. "I want him dead!" he moaned. "It was for him.... Don't you see?! You never drink tomato juice! It looked too much like blood! Don't you remember?! I put it in *his* tomato juice... I wanted to kill him! I was trying to kill Max! But you! Goodddd, Don-nie!!!" Pretty Boy was staring at the sweat on Donnie's brow. "You... drunk... it! And I've killed you! Oh God! Don-nie...."

Unable to control the shaking, trying to control the car, Donnie's mind suddenly did become crystal clear. He had heard every word. He remembered turning up the carton of tomato juice just as he went out the door when he left Max their last time. It suddenly seemed like so long ago. But in that instant, he knew what time it was. He knew Max was not at the cabin, and he knew Pretty Boy had loved him—to death.

In that instant, with a faint smile at the corner of his mouth at what to him felt was the irony of his life, he lifted a shaking finger and gently touched a tear rolling down Pretty Boy's face. And they looked into each other's eyes just for a moment.

Then, Donnie gunned the engine and turned the steering wheel of the Mercedes as far to the left as it could go.

177

He heard Pretty Boy screaming as the vehicle tumbled over the guard rail and down the cliff, tumbling, tumbling, and tumbling some more, until Donnie, lying on his back, felt like he was floating in space somewhere—staring out at the stars. It was like he could see Max's face out there in the starry black sky.

Now, he could hear nothing, save the beating of his heart—bump-bump… bump-bump…… bump—bump…….. bump——bump………..

"Max…." he whispered with his last breath.

And then, Donnie Soledad Williams could hear nothing at all.

Chapter XXV

The pain in his gut suddenly become sharper when Max drove pass the yellow tape tied onto the mangled guard rail where the SUV had plummeted over the cliff. It was a dreadful anticipation that consumed him as he drove in and out of the sun and the shadows of the trees and the curves of the mountainous route, nearing Donnie's cabin.

Was there days like this when Donnie drove up here... coming to me? He wondered. *Oh God! Did he see how beautiful it is?!* He heard himself breathing, deeply, trying to stave back the tears. *Oh God... just let me get there! Just let me .... one more time.*

Soon, he turned onto the graveled, tree-lined drive that led to the front of the cabin. He could see it through the trees. And when it came into full view, Max's body was filled with a warmth like he hadn't felt since he left the Lodge over three months ago. Another car sat in the spot where Donnie usually parked. Somewhere in the back of his mind he recognized it. Still, his hand touched the cold hood as he stood for a minute, just taking in the beauty of the Lodge.

This is where I would stand when he was leaving... wanting to go with him... waiting, until he was gone.

Since he left the Lodge, he could never bring himself to throw away the key, although he never used it when he lived there. He unlocked the front door, and went inside.

The smell of the Lodge overtook him so immediately, that he had to lean against the door with his eyes closed, breathing deeply, taking it in. It was Donnie's smell, and he wanted to take in every bit of it.

Soon he was feeling the weight, the dread overtaking him once more. He felt cold, and shivered. Opening his eyes and looking about the Lodge, he felt he couldn't move. Pushing himself away from the door, he opened the coat closet and found a leather jacket there.

"Donnie," he whispered as he caressed it. Taking it off the hanger, "Donnie," he cried, softly, and put the jacket on.

Now he was able to walk and he moved about the Lodge, while memories of love and love-making filled every room.

God! It was soooo good here! Donnie?! Why did you give me away/! Why couldn't you just let me stay? Why?!

Max slowly opened the door to the bedroom, certain that it like the rest of the cabin, still smelled of Donnie. He felt a need to fall upon the bed and bury his face in the pillow... Donnie and his pillows, just to surround himself with his smell and take him in once more, and cry.

"Sharon?!" he asked, totally surprised to see her sitting quietly on *their* bed, with pictures spread out all around her. Holding a photograph in one hand, she reached over and turned a recorder she had been listening to, off.

"Hello Max," she said, barely looking up from the photographs. "I guess I've been expecting you. What took you so long?" she asked, and placed the picture in a nearby purse.

"I was in Brazil... then, I went on a two-week sabbatical in the Andes," Max's voice trembled. "I didn't know until I got back to Sao Paw, two days ago," he explained.

"Well, this is all yours now." Now she looked at him. "My... you've changed," she said, and Max noticed there were none of the inflections he remembered in her voice.

"Yes, I've.... What are....?! How?!"

Max was coming toward her.

"Why... am I here?" Sharon finished his question. Then she took the bottle of wine sitting on the nightstand and topped off her half filled glass. She took a sip of wine, then, setting the glass down, carefully, she patted a spot on the bed motioning for him to take a seat near her. "I guess I do owe you an explanation," she said, finally.

Max took a seat on the bed in the spot where she had motioned.

"What do you mean?!" he asked.

Sharon handed him a photograph.

"When did I.... I didn't! Who is this?" he finally asked.

"That's the question," she said, and took another sip. "You want some of this?" she asked, holding the bottle up.

"Yea…. I want to know what this is all about," Max said. "What happened to Donnie?! Who is this person?" he asked. "Why are you here?!"

"Like you… I loved Donnie," she said, simply, handing Max the bottle. "All the people who loved Donnie have come here, Max. Didn't you know that?"

He didn't answer. He took the bottle.

"I'm Trey's mother," she continued, and watched her words make his face ashen. "You did realize Trey had a mother, didn't you, Max?" she asked, curiously.

Suddenly his mouth was dry. He could hardly believe what he was hearing. And still, so many questions were filling his head at the same time. He turned up the bottle of wine and took several large swallows before he could speak.

"You and… you loved Donnie? You were his wife?!" he asked.

"No… we were never married, Max. But I loved him," she replied. "And you loved Donnie… Donnie…" she smiled slightly, "… and all his lovers. Everybody lov…."

"Who… who is this?" Max asked, holding up the picture she had given him.

"That is the reason I gave you to him, darling. I knew he'd love you…. Because… that is the one other man I believe he loved. That's his dad…. His biological father," she explained. "You see, this is how I remember him looking just before he left Donnie, and his mother…. I've known Donnie all my life, it seems." She was reminiscing now, and Max was enthralled in her story.

Now, Max turned the bottle up. His legs felt like lead, but he forced himself to get up and go to the closet bar for another one. His hand shook as he uncorked it.

Looking at the old picture, so many of his questions were answered. He knew exactly what she meant when she said, *I knew he'd love you.* He was amazed at how much he once looked like the man in the photograph.

"We were just little kids back then…" she continued, "… trying to learn about the world… and life. We grew up in the same neighborhood, we went to school together. We used to play together… and we would talk about everything. Everybody just knew we'd be together… forever…. Then Donnie's dad left and his mom… well, she remarried, and nothing was ever the same again.

"The first time we were together, I got pregnant." She was gathering the photographs of her, Donnie and Trey, and some other people Max didn't recognize, and placing them in a box. "It wasn't a good time for him at home, you know. His stepfather was a.. *sick* man," she continued talking as she did this, and somehow Max felt he instinctively knew what she meant by the way she said the word, *sick*. "Anyway, he was on his way off to college... a sports scholarship, thank goodness."

She finished putting the photos in the box. Then, she finished her glass of wine. Now, she looked at Max. "Anyway," she said, and he knew she was ending. "He was not only beautiful, he was brilliant, Max. Did you know that?"

Without waiting for a reply, "I mean, his mind. He could have been an engineer... a scholar... anything, before he got fucked up! And, that bastard-man started it," she finished, stood up and took the box of photographs into her arms.

"I believe he loved me, Max.... I know he loved Trey, in his own way. But he loved *you* best. He loved you more... maybe even more than he ever loved him," she said, nodding toward the picture of Donnie's father Max still had in his hand. "Donnie came to me after he got your letter... the first one. He refused to open the other ones, Max. It was too painful for him. He was scared he'd break down and wouldn't be able to stay away from you if he read your letters or talked to you. So he stopped reading them, and he changed the telephone numbers to his place."

"If he loved me so much," Max said, "...why did he send me away?" A tear rolled down his cheek.

Now she came to him and wiped the tear from his face almost like Donnie had done to Pretty Boy.

"You really don't know, do you?!" she asked, a hint of amazement in her voice.

Max was perplexed, and his face showed it.

"Here I am, angry with you because you wasn't here... angry at Donnie... angry at the world.... And you didn't even know!"

"Know what?" Max asked.

"Know what I know," she said. "Donnie had AIDS, Max."

Max doubled over, clutching his stomach!

How can she say that?! "Wha...?!" *Breathe! Just breathe!* He felt Sharon's hand on his back, comforting, as she continued.

"He sent you away so he wouldn't give it to you."

Max crumbled down onto the bed, drained of blood and strength, unable to speak and feeling only the pain of what felt like a knife turning in his gut.

STOP!! Don't tell me any more! Can't you see? It's killing me! I'm dying! I'm dying....

But, Sharon continued: "I know he killed himself..... Donnie... and Pretty Boy," she said, finishing.

She was heading for the door. When she reached it, she stopped and turned, remembering something.

"Oh!" she said. "You remember how everything was wired... cameras... recorders. He had the SUV wired with both. The camera was destroyed in the accident." She motioned to the recorder she had switched off when Max came into the bedroom. "Somehow, the recorder got thrown clear.... They found it near Donnie's body. There's something on it, for you," she said.

Then, she left, closing the door behind her.

Max stumbled into the bathroom and emptied his gut in the toilet. Feeling too weak and too miserable to move, he lay his face down onto the cool marble floor, and closed his eyes.

Lying there, he felt Donnie's hand once more, drying the water from his nude, wet body as he met him with a towel when he stepped out of the bath on cool summer days.

Donnie's touch brought Max erotically up against the bathroom wall as he lifts his arms, lovingly, allowing Donnie to dry them, in turn. Then Donnie brings the towel down and his hands cup Max's ample, heaving breasts. Now he's kissing them, lavishly, greedily!

"Ooaahhhh, Donnie...." Max sighs, as together they slide down to the cool marble floor.

And now his legs are over Donnie's shoulders and Donnie is in him—all the way.

"Oohhh Donnie!.... Donnie!.... God!!!" Max cried.

He had no idea of how long he had been laying there. When he opened his eyes darkness surrounded him.

This whole thing has been a dream...some horrible, awful dream! But....

He sat up, feeling the cold marble beneath him.

It's not a dream! Donnie's dead. Donnie killed himself? Huh?!

He pulled himself up to his feet.

How can I say that?! I can't say that!........ Tape! She said... a tape!

He stumbled to the bed and flopped himself down onto it in the same place where he had found Sharon sitting.

Then he turned on the recorder.

Epilogue

Max staggered out onto the veranda past the steaming Jacuzzi where he and Donnie had made love that first day there. In the dark, he walked as far as his legs would carry him. And, when his legs could move no more, he stood, reeling—his chest, swelling—his heart, breaking. Still, all he could hear was it pounding ever louder!

Shouldn't it stop beating, now?! Stop! P-L-E-A-S-E STOP!

"Max...." he heard Donnie's voice as clear as it had been on the tape, and he knew he would never stop hearing Donnie whisper his name. He didn't ever want to stop hearing Donnie whisper his name.

Max threw his head back, staring into that same black, star-spangled sky that Donnie's eyes had last seen; and, summoning all the strength left in him, as if calling his love back from the stars, he yelled:

"DON-NIE!!!"

Before he fell to his knees wanting never to get up, again.

The End

185